# CHRISTMAS A.N.G.E.L.S

## C.J. PETERSON

ISBN - 978-1-952041-48-8 (paperback)

# CONTENTS

# SUMMARY

**Novella: *Christmas A.N.G.E.L.s:***

Life as an A.N.G.E.L. has always been hectic but rewarding for Rachel English. However, sometimes you need to stop and reevaluate life. With two kids and a set of twins due any minute, along with the holidays coming, her brother's wedding, and being in charge of both American A.N.G.E.L. teams…it's too much for Rachel. Take a journey of the heart and soul with her as she has to make a life-altering decision.

**Bonus Story: *Christmas Wish:***

For six-year-old Robin Flynn and her family, this is a Christmas that will change everything. There will be treats, a wish for a healthy delivery of Robin's new brother, and a mother's wish for her son to move on from the past. A kindhearted Pastor is sent to help the family navigate through the turmoil that arose on this Christmas Eve night. Will all their Christmas wishes come true?

# Christmas A.N.G.E.L.s

C.J. Peterson

"*R*achel, I have an idea," Angel said, walking into Rachel's office in the basement. She sat in the chair across from Rachel. Tucking a portion of her hazelnut brown hair behind her ear, she then nervously nibbled on her nails as she studied Rachel with her green eyes.

"What's up?" Rachel asked. Rachel still had her Australian accent, despite living in Nevada for several years. Rachel was *Overwatch* over both of the American teams.

"Well, with the double wedding coming up two days before Christmas, I wanted to plan a special Christmas present for the couples."

"What do you have in mind?" Rachel asked, sitting back in her seat. Her eight-month pregnancy left her exhausted most days by noon. She and Jesse had two children, Charles Nicholas (Charlie) and Derek Mark. With both Rachel and Jesse being twins themselves, it was no surprise to them when the doctor told them this pregnancy was a set of twins. The babies were fraternal – a girl and a boy. Rachel and Jesse decided to name them: Katherine Elizabeth (Katie) and Ethan Allen. She was due a week after the weddings were to take place.

Everyone knew the scheduling would be close, but the two couples had their hearts set on a Christmas wedding, and they waited long enough. Both couples waited over six months to get married.

Working together, the A.N.G.E.L.s naturally formed couples over the years. Some worked out, some did not. Either way, they all remained friends and had good working relationships. A.N.G.E.L. stands for - Available to Nurture God's Eternal Love. There are units or teams all over the world. These teams get their assignments from Michael the Archangel, who sends them throughout the world to help people. Sometimes they got to the person they were sent to help in time…sometimes they did not. Whatever they did, they gave everything they had for the Lord. The Lord also bestowed each A.N.G.E.L. with a unique spiritual gift. These gifts allowed the A.N.G.E.L.s to see what could not be readily seen, to feel what they could not see, and to anticipate what was ahead.

The couples on the American A.N.G.E.L. teams had great success when it came to marriages. Angel and Sasha got married a year ago. She is expecting her first child in five months. Jacob and Cori got married three years ago. They are happily married, and have recently started trying to have children. The group has been waiting for them to tell them they were pregnant, but nothing yet. Joe and Delaney got married a year and a half ago. They decided to wait a bit to have children. They wanted to enjoy each other before children came into their lives.

The two couples getting married were Josh and Zahra, and Spencer and Katia. Val and Katia broke up a year and a half ago. She and Spencer started dating a few months later. Val was hurt, but he understood how different he and Katia were at their core. He wished them nothing but the best when he found out Spencer proposed to Katia and Katia accepted. Meanwhile, once Josh finally asked Zahra out, they were inseparable.

With two couples engaged, they thought it would be

wonderful to have a double wedding. So, the group got together and the planning commenced.

"What's your idea?" Rachel asked, when Angel did not respond.

"Not sure how to word it," she said, uneasily.

"If you have an idea, you have to tell me what's going through that brain of yours. I love you, but I'm not a mind reader."

"True," Angel said. "Okay, bear with me while I explain it. Please understand my line of thinking."

Rachel flipped her blonde hair up into a ponytail. She narrowed her blue eyes at Angel, as she asked, "Why are you being so squirrely?"

"Because I don't know how this is going to be received. I also know you're going to have to figure out how to talk to your parents about what I'm proposing."

"Okay. Enough, Angel. I don't have time for games. Just tell me what you need?"

"I want to get the families together for the weddings."

"And?"

"And, you remember Spencer's mom, Stacey, and your mom have a past."

"Oh." Rachel nodded. "That *could* cause an issue."

"Spencer said he understands why his parents can't come to the wedding. However, he was one of my best friends in college. I know how much his parents mean to him. I also know how much your parents mean to Josh. I think both sets of parents should be there. I think it would mean the world to both of them."

"I understand. However, his parents think my mum is dead. To Stacey, my mum was killed by a mafia boss over thirty years ago. When she comes walking into the wedding, pretty sure Stacey will have a heart attack thinking she saw a ghost."

"That's why I wanted to talk to you," Angel explained. "It's

Christmas. It's a time to celebrate. It's also a time of giving. It's a time of reconciliation. It's a time of family coming together. Look, I'm pretty sure Stacey and Scott would keep Kit and Nico's secret. Do you really think there's still a threat on her life at this point? As for Spencer, he doesn't have any siblings. If we only invite Stacey and Scott, no other friends or family, and make sure they understand the situation, I'm sure they'll comply."

Rachel debated for a few moments. "Let me talk to Mum and Dad first. Don't mention it to anyone else."

Angel grinned as a thrill of excitement charged through her. "Agreed! Thank you!"

After Angel left her office, Rachel sighed before she called out, "Hey, Cori!"

"What do ya need?" Cori asked, from her position at the computer.

"Please get my Mum and Dad on the line?"

⁂

"I DUNNO," Nico said over the phone once Rachel explained what she wanted. He was on one phone, while Kit was on another. They both sat on the bed in their room.

"There are a couple things to consider," Rachel explained. "It's been years since anyone even remotely looked into Mum. Cori's flagged your name, so anyone looking for you would trigger a notification and we would know. Another thing is Spencer is Scott and Stacey's only child. To make them miss this isn't fair. As for you? I can't imagine you really want to miss Josh's wedding either?"

"I don't want to miss it," Kit admitted. "It's bad enough we're on the other side of the world from you two. I would also love to see Stacey, but she thinks I'm dead."

"What if I talk to Scott and Stacey before they come?"

Rachel asked. "I could have them sign a non-disclosure statement?"

Nico stroked his chin. "That may not be a bad idea."

"Nico!" Kit said, appalled. "Is that a serious consideration? You would make them sign one of those things?"

"Of course. Why not?"

"I cannot believe you would make them do that!"

"Mum, it's for your safety," Rachel explained. "Not to mention the safety of the A.N.G.E.L.s. It's not just your secret we're protecting here."

"How exactly are you planning on talking to them?" Kit asked. "Are you going to wait until they get there? You know what? Never mind. I don't want this to be an issue. What if we just don't come?"

"That's *not* an option. We're going!" Nico insisted. "I'm not missing the birth of two more grandkids, nor am I missing Josh's wedding. I think it'll be fine if Rachel talks to them first."

"We've kept it a secret for this long," Kit said.

"I thought you and Stacey were close in college?" Rachel asked. "Weren't you in her wedding?"

"Yes," Kit said.

"Wouldn't you like to see her again?"

"I would, but –"

"Then, it looks like you're all coming to our house for the holidays!" Rachel said. "No more arguments."

"All right," Kit relented. "We'll do it."

"I don't think this is a good idea," Jesse said to Rachel as they picked up their luggage at the airport in Cleveland, Ohio. They each had a carry-on and a small pull-behind suitcase. Afterward, they headed toward the taxi waiting for them outside the airport.

"Why not?" Rachel asked. "Imagine you're an only child. Would you not want your parents at your wedding?"

"Yes."

"Now, pretend you're Josh. Wouldn't you want Mum and Dad there?"

"Yes, but –"

"No buts. Angel had a good idea. I agree with her. We need to do this for Josh *and* Spencer. As it is, Zahra can't have her family there, and Katia doesn't have any family except yours and Liliya. At the very least, we need to grant them this one wish. Besides, it would bring my mum some cheer to see her friend Stacey again. C'mon, grant everyone this Christmas wish?"

"All right." Jesse gave up. "Just please take it easy. Pete would kill me if something happened to you. He didn't want you to fly. It took Nico to convince him to let you come here."

"I'm glad he's been able to be here for the pregnancy."

"This has been a difficult one for you."

"I know. I promise to take it easy. Is that our taxi?" Rachel pointed to a car waiting.

"Yep." They walked over. While Jesse and the driver put the bags in the trunk, Rachel got into the backseat. "This address in Pine Crest, please?" Jesse said, handing the driver the address, and then he slid in the backseat beside Rachel.

"No problem, sir," he said. "Just know it's a good forty-five minutes."

"We know. Thank you," Jesse acknowledged.

After paying the driver and gathering their luggage, Jesse and Rachel stood in front of Scott and Stacey Schmidt's home in Pine Crest, Ohio. The Schmidt home was a white, two-story colonial house with a red door. With it being the beginning of December, the home was already decorated for Christmas. There were wreathes in each window facing the street, with a battery-operated candle resting in the center of each wreath. They could see the nine-foot tree with white lights through the windows. It was ordained with old-fashioned ornaments, along red, green, and silver ribbons, and silver beads for garland.

As they stood there, Rachel wrapped her coat tighter around body when a cold winter breeze whipped by, sweeping more snow into the street. With six-inches of snow already down, the extra four inches expected would complete the winter wonder-land scene.

"My dad told me stories about this town," Rachel said, looking around. "It used to be a horrific town to live in from the point it was founded. I guess the founding families pretty much ruled the town. There was a battle over thirty years ago that finally released them from the stronghold. Stacey and her dad were part of the battle to release them."

"All I feel right now is peace," Jesse observed.

"That's all that's left," Rachel agreed. "Well, let's go. It's not getting any warmer."

Jesse shivered. "Man! I really miss the warm Nevada weather."

"We'll head back in a few days. Until then, enjoy the beauty that is winter in the northeast."

Together, they headed up the walkway to the front door.

"I wish Spencer could come with us," Jesse mentioned, as he pressed the doorbell.

"We're couldn't in case they didn't sign the paperwork. It's also meant to be a surprise for him."

"This is going to be interesting," Jesse said under his breath.

The door opened. There was an older woman who stood to about five foot nine or ten, same as Rachel. She looked to be about Rachel's mom's age. She had blonde hair and blue eyes. "Jesse and Rachel?" Stacey asked.

"Yep!" Rachel said, shaking her hand.

"Welcome! Come in! Come in! Scott'll be back shortly. He ran to the store for a few items," Stacey explained, as she grabbed their carry-ons to bring in with her.

"Thank you for letting us stay with you," Jesse said. "We really appreciate it."

"We're happy to have you," she said. "How's Spencer? We get a few emails here and there, but not a lot of details."

"He's not allowed to give details," Jesse explained.

"I know. We understand. It's evident he's happy. That's all we can ask."

"Stacey," Scott called, as he walked into the kitchen from the garage with several grocery bags hanging off his arms.

"In here!" she called back. Together the three of them headed into the kitchen. "Do you need help?" Stacey asked.

"Nope. This is it. You must be Jesse and Rachel?" Scott asked, setting the bags on the counter. As Stacey set to emptying them, Scott introduced himself to Rachel and Jesse.

"Yes. Thank you for having us," Jesse said, shaking his hand.

"Not a problem at all," Scott said. "Happy to have you. Spencer doing okay?"

"Yes. He loves what he's doing," Jesse said.

"That's obvious when we talk to him. Just wish we knew more."

Rachel took her coat off. "Um, funny you should mention that."

"Oh! My word!" Stacey realized how large Rachel was, and ushered Rachel into the living room. "Please sit down. You must be exhausted. How far along are you? Here, let me take your coats," she said, and rested both of their coats over a chair in the dining room before returning to the living room beside Scott.

"I'm eight months. I'm due on the thirtieth of December. They're twins," she said, sitting on the couch with Jesse beside her, while Scott and Stacey sat on the couch opposite them.

"What do you mean funny we should mention wanting to know more about what he does?" Scott asked, his curiosity piqued.

"That's the reason we're here," Rachel explained. "We want to tell you everything, but we can't unless you sign these non-disclosure agreements," she said, pulling them out of her bag. She set the paperwork on the coffee table between the couples.

"Does he work for homeland security or something?" Scott asked, thumbing through the paperwork. "There is a lot of legal speak in this. Maybe we should let your dad read this?" he suggested to Stacey.

Stacey picked it up and looked through it. "It's actually pretty standard stuff."

"How would you know?" Scott asked.

"Scott, I work as a profiler for the FBI. Trust me. I've seen these more than enough times," Stacey said. She went to the kitchen and grabbed a pen. "I have no problem signing this."

When Stacey came back into the living room, Rachel explained, "You cannot say anything to anyone about what we're going to tell you, including the government."

"Really?" she asked, wide-eyed, as she sat back down next to Scott. "You're not going to tell us something that could get us in legal trouble, are you?"

"No. No. Not at all. As a matter of fact, my dad used to work spec ops for the Air Force," Jesse explained. "We keep every-thing above board. There are just certain things we need to keep under wraps."

"All right," Stacey said, signing the paperwork. When she finished, she handed Scott the pen. "Your turn."

"Are you sure about this?" Scott asked.

"Do you want to find out what Spencer's doing for real?" Stacey challenged.

"Fine," Scott said on a sigh. As he signed the paperwork, he said, "You'd better not get us arrested."

"You'll be fine," Rachel said. After tucking the signed paper-work into her bag, she explained, "Spencer works for us. We're a team called A.N.G.E.L., which stands for: Available to Nurture God's Eternal Love. We get our assignments from Michael, the Archangel. He sends us all over the world to help people. The American team has two teams, both of which I am over. They call me Overwatch. The house, which is near Reno, Nevada, houses both teams. Each team has a group which stays at the house as support. The house is called The Safe Haven – or Haven for short. The other team members go out into the field."

Scott raised an eyebrow. "Are you serious?"

"Yes. Very," Rachel said. "Your son is part of the group which is generally at the Haven. However, there are times he is needed in the field. He helps in many aspects, from the lab to archeological field work."

"Interesting," Stacey said. "We had no idea. We knew it was some type of lab work. Is he safe in the field?"

"He is under the direct supervision of Michael the Archangel," Rachel explained. "As one of his A.N.G.E.L.s, we all are."

"I'm having a difficult time wrapping my brain around this one. Are you being straight with us or is this a joke?" Scott asked. "You actually work for an Archangel of the Lord God?"

"Yes," Rachel said.

Scott shook his head. "I'm sorry. I'm having a really hard time accepting what you're telling me."

"I'm not," Stacey said. "Remember Kyle?"

"Who could forget him?" Scott rolled his eyes. "That kid was pure evil!"

"Right. He could put you into some kind of trance, and make you doubt everything you ever knew," Stacey explained. "We've seen first-hand how evil can rule. We also know the Archangel Michael is real. He's in the Bible. Why would you doubt what they're telling us?"

"I know Jesus, God, and the Spirit are real. I know demons and Satan are real," Scott said. "I am having a hard time wrapping my mind around the fact that all of this stuff is going on literally in this world."

"Oh! It is," Rachel assured him. "Now, the reason we explained all of this is because, as you know, Spencer and his lady are close."

"Right. He hasn't been able to tell us much about her, though," Stacey explained.

"Her name is Katia. She grew up in Russia. We picked her up several years ago for our team. She and her sister are each on a team and have been adopted by Jesse's family. Katia does field work, while her sister, Liliya, works at the Haven and goes in the field occasionally as medical. Katia is a sweet lady. She and Spencer are a great match. You're going to meet them."

"What? When?" Stacey asked.

"I didn't think we could," Scott said, still trying to process everything.

"That's why we had you sign the paperwork," Jesse explained. Then he handed them their tickets. "You fly out on the twentieth of December. Now, we know your schedules are tough, so we've done a little backroom scheming."

Scott narrowed his eyes. "What does that mean?"

"Well, Stacey, you are going to be given a secret mission from your home office. You will receive the orders tomorrow," Jesse explained. "Meanwhile, Scott, your Chief will receive notice you are required to do a training in Texas, which starts the twenty-first, so you will be off that entire week."

"How did you swing that one?" Scott asked, dumbfounded.

"We have very good people who work for us," Rachel said with a twinkle in her eyes.

"Okay, then," Scott said. Turning to Stacey, he added, "Looks like we're going to Nevada for Christmas."

A look of pure joy spread across Stacey's face. Then a thought hit her. "Can my dad and Becky come?"

"No." Rachel shook her head. "Just the two of you. You have to make your choice now."

"Oh! We're going," Scott said. "That's not in question. We haven't seen Spencer in over six years."

"I agree. I'm just...can we take pictures?" Stacey asked. "I mean pictures of the wedding and of Spencer?"

"Unfortunately, no," Rachel said. "You may inadvertently get someone else in the picture. Besides, as far as the world is concerned, Spencer doesn't exist anymore."

"True," Stacey said. "He did mention that, and I can't find him with my contacts anymore. I just hate that we don't have any pictures of him. I miss him. When I do, I at least had older pictures of him from college to lean on."

Understanding where Stacey's heart was, Rachel said,

"Maybe we can get a picture of just the three of you. Katia cannot be in the picture. I'll have Callie take it with her 35mm film camera and develop it there. You cannot show it to anyone, though."

"I promise!" Stacey said, excited. "I can't wait!"

"Now, about those little ones," Scott said, referring to Rachel's pregnancy. "When are you due again?

# DECK THE HALLS

Rachel and Jesse returned to a flurry of activity. Normally, the Haven is organized chaos. However, with two weddings and Rachel's pregnancy, it made the chaos levels jump ten-fold for the next few weeks.

Finally, the day arrived where Kit, Nico, and their family flew into Nevada from Queensland, Australia. It took Josh and Jon each driving a fifteen-passenger van to get the entire family back to the Haven. Nico and Kit were in Jon's van, along with Rachel's twin sister, Leah, her husband, Finn Walker, and their children: Sophie (seven years old), Piper (five years old), Elijah (four years old), Sebastian (two years old), and four-month-old, Conner. Meanwhile, in Josh's van were his twin brother, Caleb, Caleb's wife, Willow, and their children: Jasper (fifteen years old), twins Benjamin and Lily (twelve years old), and Zachary (nine years old). Needless to say, their vans were full! Thankfully, the Haven was ready for them. There was an entire wing set up for guests. This was normally designated for other A.N.G.E.L. teams when they came in for visits through the years, but for a few weeks, it would house the families.

After the chaos of everyone arriving and getting settled, two of Rachel's nephews sat down on either side of her. "So," Jasper said, "who are the exotic beauties in the kitchen with Auntie Casey?"

"That's Allie and Callie," Rachel said. "They're Mark and Casey's girls."

"They don't look like Uncle Mark or Auntie Casey," Ben pointed out.

"They're the twins we rescued back when they were being held by the other side at Black Rock," Rachel explained. "Their mum died during the rescue, so Mark and Casey adopted them. You haven't seen them, because we never brought them with us back to the station."

"How old are they?" Jasper asked. Then he glanced into the kitchen to get another good look at them. "They are seriously fine young ladies."

"Jasper Dylan!" Rachel said, stunned.

"What? I have eyes!" Jasper defended himself. "They're hot!"

"Goodness!" Rachel rolled her eyes. "You're incorrigible!"

"I'm a fifteen-year-old boy," Jasper said. "Seriously, how old are they?"

Rachel sighed. "They're fourteen."

"Hmm," Jasper said, looking at them again. "Maybe I'll connect with them."

"You know, that's only two years older than me," Ben pointed out. "I could be your wingman."

"Ben!" Rachel said, shocked. "I cannot believe the two of you."

"Have you *seen* them?" Ben asked. "They're a couple of hot sheilas."

"Just be kind. If you hurt them in any way, I promise you there will be nowhere on this planet to hide," Rachel warned. "They are the little sisters to every resident in this home. That's not even including the other A.N.G.E.L.s of the world."

Jasper raised his hands in surrender. "Enough said. We'll be good."

"How about you just be friends with them?" Rachel asked. "You can connect on a friend level. Leave the hooking up with the sheilas back in Australia."

"We'll just go have a chat," Ben said, as he and Jasper got off the couch, meandering into the kitchen.

When they were gone, Jerrod, one of the older A.N.G.E.L.s, who was also a former Corpsman in the Navy, sat on the coffee table across from Rachel. "Rach, you only have two weeks left until these two little ones come. You've got your hands full with their delivery coming, along with your other two little ones. That's not even mentioning the weddings."

"I know. I'm doing my best," Rachel said, propping her feet onto the coffee table as the kids and other family and team members buzzed around the Haven.

"Frankly, I'm not exactly sure how you're still standing. I know for a fact you've been having contractions, but haven't told anyone. I can see it on your face."

"Jesse knows. I can't hide anything from him," Rachel admitted.

"What does he say about it?"

"He's leaving it up to me. He said he's confident I'll make the right decisions."

"Can I make a suggestion?" Jerrod asked.

"What?"

"Let me step up. You know I can handle it. I did for a bit when you had your other kids. I know how things work. Having two at once is going to be a bigger challenge than you're used to."

"I know. Mum and Willow already warned me of that."

"Then?"

"Fine. I'll work on getting ready for the weddings and leave the A.N.G.E.L. business to you."

"Actually, leave it all. You're supposed to be in the wedding, but I am really not seeing that happen," Jared pointed out. "At this point, if you make your due date, I'll be stunned."

"You reckon?"

"Rach, take a really good look at yourself. Your ankles are swollen. You are exhausted by lunch. You have two other little ones to keep track of, while trying to juggle the A.N.G.E.L.s. Allowing me to step up to take the A.N.G.E.L.s off your hands for a bit will alleviate some of the pressure, but you have to give up control or you're going to lose it completely."

"Fine," Rachel said on a sigh. "I'll just keep track of the little guys. Speaking of which…where *are* Charlie and Derek?"

"They're playing with the other kids out back. Don't worry about them. The others will look after them. Seriously, get some rest while you still can. Maybe work on Christmas presents? Do something fun."

"Right oh," Rachel relented. "After I sit down with Mum and Dad, I'll go for a kip."

"Good idea. I'll go get them," Jared said, and then left for the kitchen.

"Rachel?" Kai poked his head out the basement door.

"What's up, Kai?"

"Joe, Delaney, and Jacob are trying to get back in time for the weddings, but they've run into a snag."

Rachel groaned as she struggled to get off the couch.

"Stay there," Jerrod ordered. "I got it." With that, they disappeared into the basement.

"Rachel!" Akio called from the basement.

"I got it!" Jerrod yelled from the basement.

Rachel dropped back onto the couch. "Thank you!"

"Mummy!" Charlie ran into the living room, quickly followed by Derek. "Derek took my car and won't give it back."

"I did not! It's mine!" Derek shouted, clutching the precious car.

Liliya came into the living room. "I got this," she said. "Come on, guys." She picked up Derek and carried him out to the back porch, with Charlie on her heels.

Rachel sighed as she looked up at the ceiling. "Sometimes I wish this chaos wasn't our world," she said in a whispered prayer. "I know You've blessed us all these years, but there are times where I wish it wasn't so stressful."

"So, I hear you have some news for us?" Nico asked, as he and Kit sat on the couch with Rachel.

"Yes. I wanted to tell you we told Scott and Stacey everything *except* about you, Mum. We decided that would be better explained when you're face-to-face," Rachel said.

"This is true," Kit agreed. "I'm sure it will be a shock."

"Also, Jared is taking over the A.N.G.E.L.s starting now, until a few months after the babies are born."

"You haven't told us what you're going to name them," Nico said. "Do we have to wait until they're born to find out?"

"No. We wanted to tell you when you got here. Jesse!" Rachel yelled.

Jesse came running up from the basement. "Yeah?" he asked, poking his head out the door.

"Mum and Dad want to know the names of the babies," Rachel said.

"Oh. Okay. Just a sec," he said, and disappeared back downstairs. He returned a few minutes later with Josh, Zahra, Jon, Mark, Casey, Leah, Finn, Caleb, Willow, with Josh and Jessie lifting Derek and his wheelchair up the stairs. They were all downstairs looking around at what was updated since their last visit. Jerrod was still downstairs with the remaining team members sorting out issues.

Once everyone was settled, and Derek had a good spot in his wheelchair, Nico said, "Well, the gang's all here."

"And it's standing-room only," Jesse added with a smile.

"Rachel, go ahead and tell them." He sat beside her on the couch as Nico moved to the coffee table across from her.

"Well, you know Charlie is named after Charlie and you, Dad," Rachel said to Nico taking Jesse's hand into hers. When he nodded, she continued, "Then, Derek is named after Derek, and Mark." Mark and Derek nodded, so Rachel continued, "These two are boy and girl twins. So, we're naming the boy Ethan, after the Colonel, and Mark and Jesse's middle name, Allen." That announcement was met with delight. Rachel then added, "And, the girl will be named Katherine after you, Mum, and my middle name, Elizabeth."

"Aww! Really?" Kit gushed.

"Yes," Rachel said. "We're going to call her Katie for short."

Kit gave her hug. Everyone was thrilled with their choice.

"Are you guys going to have more?" Leah asked.

"No." Rachel shook her head. "I'm getting my tubes tied and Jesse's already been...*fixed*," she admitted, with her face flushed red. "Four is enough."

"Well, I can honestly say our quiver is full," Kit said. "We have been blessed with four beautiful children. Those children all chose incredible spouses to be their partners in life. Each couple is strong in the Lord, and all have a large brood of their own. We couldn't ask for anything more!"

"Except that we're just starting," Josh pointed out, wrapping his arms around Zahra from behind. "We'll still need to add ours to the mix."

"I cannot wait!" Zahra grinned. "My family cannot be here for the wedding. I cannot have contact with them, because it is not safe."

"Well, as you can see, you have more than enough family here," Kit said, giving her a hug as well.

"Not to mention the family she has with the other A.N.G.E.L.s," Jon added.

"Yes. We are all blessed here," Zahra said. "God grants us

many blessings." Zahra was from Egypt. She had the dark skin, hair, and eyes reminiscent of Egyptians. Meanwhile, Jon was her polar opposite. With is fair skin, blonde hair, and blue eyes, along with his six-foot-four height, he stood out in a crowd.

"Yes. He has," Casey said. "And over the years, He has blessed us beyond measure on so many levels. Speaking of blessings, there are cookies to decorate for the little blessings," Casey announced. "Allie, Callie, and I have been cooking all day. That will give the little ones plenty to do. The guys are supposed to get the tree later. That leaves the popcorn to string, and the decorations put up around the house. We waited until you all got here, so we could all participate."

"I think that's a marvelous idea!" Kit said. "So much to do!"

"There's a lot of grocery shopping to do as well," Casey pointed out. "We still have two more people coming."

"Then, let's go deck the halls!" Jesse said, getting off the couch.

"I'm going for a kip, if that's okay?" Rachel asked.

"Definitely," Jesse said, helping her off the couch. "A nap will do you some good."

"Here," Pete said, coming into the living room with a cup of tea. When she raised an eyebrow, he blushed as he explained, "You seem a little stressed."

"Thank you." Rachel accepted the cup. She downed it before heading upstairs. Climbing into bed, she thought about the many blessings God bestowed upon the A.N.G.E.L.s. Then, as the tea took effect, her mind wondered toward the stress and chaos swirling around them. While she drifted off to sleep, she wondered what her life would have been like if the A.N.G.E.L.s were not involved.

# IT'S A WONDERFUL LIFE

"Rachel?" a nurse walked up to her at the nurse's station in the hospital.

"What?" Rachel asked, working on a report.

"Dr. Foster's changed the meds on room sixteen. He asked me to have you check his notes."

"Okay. Thanks, Millie. I'll do it when I finish here," she said.

"Rach, Dr. Walters needs you to schedule a procedure for room twenty," another nurse said, coming to the nurse's station.

"Why don't you do it?" Rachel asked.

The nurse sighed. "Because *I'm* not the head nurse. *You* are."

"Steph, go ahead and schedule it. I have to finish this report and change the meds for room sixteen."

"Can't." Steph shrugged. "Not my job," she said, and left for another room.

Rachel grunted in frustration. She quickly finished the report, and then scheduled the procedure before she changed the medication. After shift change, she was relieved to finally clock-out. It was a busy shift.

Heading home, she stopped for some grocery shopping. As she pulled into the parking lot of her condo, she felt a sense of relief wash over her. She was home. Work was stressful. She was grateful it was twelve-hour shifts for only half the week. This was the start of her long weekend.

Grabbing her mail on the way up, she longed for her bed. Unlocking the door, she was greeted by a fluffy Australian Silky Terrier. "Hi, Jesse," she said scratching the chin of her adorable six-year-old best friend. "Are you hungry?"

Jesse licked her hand.

"Good boy," she said, taking inventory of any potential damage Jesse may have executed in her absence. Grateful for the reprieve of not finding any, she ran Jesse out to go to the bathroom. Once she returned, she fed her pup his dinner, and then put hers in the oven.

She slid off her shoes. Her feet pulsated from being on them all day. She regretfully started wearing tights to stop anymore varicose veins from appearing. Due to long hours of being on her feet, they started showing up a few weeks ago. She propped her feet on the coffee table as she sunk into the couch. She did a few minutes of stretching her feet and legs until the pulsating calmed.

"Rachel?" she heard a man's voice and just about jumped out of her skin. Instead of getting up, she froze.

"Who-who are you?" Rachel stammered unable to move.

The man who stood before her looked to be about seven-feet tall. He had blonde hair and the bluest eyes she ever saw. His cheeks were ruddy, with young-looking, strong features. He stood in front of her in a chiton, with a sword hanging on his waist. While his height was terrifying, and his clothing unique, the wings which fanned out behind him sent her mind spiraling.

"Fear not, Rachel," Michael, The Archangel, said.

She gulped. "A little late for that." Glancing at Jesse, she saw him calmly eating his food as if there was not a real-life angel standing in the middle of her living room.

"You are worn-out and confused. I want to show you what it would be like if you were one of my A.N.G.E.L.s."

"What do you mean one of your A.N.G.E.L.s?" Rachel asked.

He sat on the coffee table next to her feet. Clasping his hands in front of him, he explained, "You are head of two teams. Those teams get their assignments from me. I, of course, receive them from The Lord God Almighty."

"Are you bloody serious? Have you gone 'round the twist?" she asked.

He chuckled. "No. I am not crazy. What you currently see around you, is what your life would be had the A.N.G.E.L.s not been in your life."

Rachel furrowed her brow. "Are you saying this isn't my real life? That sounds crazy."

"Tell me about what your life has been like up until this point," Michael suggested.

"Well," she started, "I grew up in a house on the beach. I have a Mum, Dad, and brother."

"What are their names?"

"Dad's name is Nathan. My Mum's name is Claire. And, my brother's name is Jake."

"And, your last name is?"

"Locke. Why?"

"Because in reality, your last name is Sullivan. You have two brothers who are twins – Joshua and Caleb. You also have a twin sister, Leah. Your parent's names are Nico and Kit."

"No."

"Yes. Your dad has a brother, right?"

"Yes. He's a twin. His brother's name is Nick."

"That's actually your dad."

"No. My dad's brother is an FBI agent in the States. Why are you saying all of this?"

"Jesse is actually your husband," Michael explained.

"I'm not married."

"Go turn off your dinner so it does not burn," Michael instructed.

Rachel got up and turned off the oven. When she turned back around, the angel was standing in front of her with his hand out.

"Take my hand," he instructed.

She took his hand. One second they were standing in her condo. The next second, they were standing in the middle of The Haven. There were children running around, laughing and playing. People were bustling about, getting ready for Christmas. Three guys brought in the Christmas tree. As soon as they set it up, the men and children decorated, while the women were in the kitchen either cleaning, cooking, or baking.

"This activity is dizzying!" Rachel remarked. "What kind of people live like this? Is it a commune or something?"

"This is the home of the American A.N.G.E.L.s," Michael explained in a chuckle regarding the *commune* comment. "It is also known as the Safe Haven."

"These are all angels?" Rachel asked.

"No. They are A.N.G.E.L.s, as in Team A.N.G.E.L.," he said, understanding her question.

"*All* of these people?" Rachel asked, astounded.

"No. Some are older A.N.G.E.L.s, such as Mark and Casey English over there. Derek Cruise is over there in the wheelchair. Then, that group over there are part of the next generation, while that group are current A.N.G.E.L.s."

"There are some really cute guys in that group," Rachel pointed toward the group of the current team.

"Any in particular?" Michael asked.

"Actually, those two guys are super cute. The one on the right stands out to me."

"That is your husband, Jesse English."

"My…*what?*" Rachel's jaw dropped.

"Even in another life, you and Jesse were connected. Do you not find the irony your dog being named Jesse?"

"Well, maybe," she said with a shrug.

"You and Jesse have been married for six years."

"Really?" she asked. "That's how old his is."

"Exactly. He has been in your life as long as you have been married. Now, do you see those two little boys playing with the cars?" Michael asked.

"Yes."

"Those two are yours. Their names are Charlie and Derek. Do you currently have children?"

"No. Just my dog."

"In this reality, you are also pregnant with twins – a boy and a girl."

"Is that me over there?" she asked, pointing toward a girl who looked identical to her.

"No. That's Leah. She is your twin sister."

"Interesting."

"Yes. Now, come. Let us go downstairs," he said, putting his elbow out. As she looped her arm through his, he explained, "Downstairs is where the hub of these two teams is located."

"I see."

They went downstairs to see the two teams bustling around. There were two computer stations, along with a lab, and a room with tables and light tables, along with camera equipment, and a door, which led to an enclosed room.

"Okay, the computer sections are obvious," Rachel said. "Even the lab is obvious. What is that room over there?" she asked, pointing to the other room.

"Well, there are times where documentation is needed in a hurry. The team members also may need a badge or something along those lines."

"Are you saying they forge documents?"

Michael smiled. "They are the best."

"All righty then," Rachel said, shaking her head. "So, what do these people do?"

"I told you –"

"You told me you send them out on assignments," she said, cutting him off. "What *kind* of assignments?"

"Assignments where either the person's soul or their lives are in need of rescuing," Michael explained.

"Okay," she said, filing the information. Then she asked, "What's that door over there?"

"That is your office," he said, and they went to the door.

"What do you mean *my* office?"

"As I said before, you are over both of these teams. You are known as Overwatch."

"Okay. Can we go in?"

"Of course!" he said, and opened the door.

She walked into a ten-by-ten-foot room. One wall was covered in book shelves. There were books, mixed with pictures in frames and music boxes from various countries.

On the wall behind the desk, there was a dry erase board with tiny magnets showing whether the team members were in or out. If they were out, it was written next to the name as to the location. The only ones currently out were Joe, Delaney, and Jacob. It said they were in Ireland.

On the third wall was the door. There was a poster on each side in a frame, with a verse. The first poster's verse was Jeremiah 29:11, which says, *'For I know the plans I have for you,"  declares the Lord, "plans to prosper you and not to harm you, plans to give you hope and a future.'* The other poster's verse was Hebrews 14:6, which says, *'Let us therefore come boldly unto the throne of grace, that we may obtain mercy, and find grace to help in time of need.'*

Rachel walked over to the desk. Picking up a picture frame, she asked, "Is this my family?"

"Yes," he said. "That was everyone who attended Leah and Finn's wedding."

The picture was at Serenity Wells Station in front of the main house. All of the ranch hands, Pete's clan members, the Sullivan's, and the A.N.G.E.L.s who were there were in the picture.

"This is my Uncle Nick's station. He lives in the States. It's run by his best mate, Pete."

"In this reality, it's run by this man," Michael pointed Caleb out in the picture.

"I thought he was upstairs?"

"He is. But the one you saw was his twin. You see, this is Nico," he said pointing him out. "In this reality, he is married to Kit," he said pointing her out. "They were also known as Nick Locke and Katie MacKenna. They have four children." He pointed to each as he said their name, "There are the older brother twins, Joshua and Caleb. Then a little while later, they had another set of twins, Rachel and Leah."

"Oh! Wait! Are you saying in this reality, my uncle is my dad?"

"Yes."

"Why is it different in my reality?"

"There are many differences between your realities. The difference is Jesus Christ and the A.N.G.E.L.s."

"What do you mean?"

"In this reality, you are exhausted and frustrated," Michael explained. "You are wondering if you are really making a difference. You are wondering if the A.N.G.E.L.s are making a difference. What you do not understand is just how much your life and the A.N.G.E.L.s are intertwined. You were all brought together through a series of events. You run across people every day. Those choices…those decisions…those meetings…they all make a difference. Even the challenges you face, make you into who you are today."

Eyebrows arched in surprise, she asked, "So, you're saying even one person could make the difference between my reality and this reality?"

"Yes," he said.

At that moment, a very pregnant Rachel walked into the office. "Okay. This is creepy," she said, looking from the other Rachel to Michael. "Michael, what's going on?"

Michael walked over to pregnant Rachel. He took her hands into his, and explained what nurse Rachel's life looked like up to that point.

When he finished, pregnant Rachel asked, "So, why is she here?"

"I am giving you a choice," he said.

"A choice as to which reality I want?" pregnant Rachel asked.

"Yes. However, I need you both to come to an agreement. Only one reality will be retained. Before you decide, please grant me some time to show you a few things so you can make an educated decision?"

Pregnant Rachel glanced at nurse Rachel, who stood there in her scrubs with her arms crossed. "Are you willing to work with me to figure out the reality we both want?" pregnant Rachel asked nurse Rachel.

"Yes," nurse Rachel said. As she made her way next to Michael, she added, "If you are willing to see my reality as well."

"Agreed."

"Good. Then, allow us to take a walk," he said putting both hands out, one toward each Rachel. After each one took a hand, they walked out into the computer lab. "We will start in here," he announced.

"How are we going to do this?" pregnant Rachel asked.

"We will begin with the crew you acquired from Ireland – Cori, Delaney, and Kai," he explained. "You see, here they are making a difference in the lives of those they save and look out for each and every day."

"They are amazing in what they do," pregnant Rachel said. "There is nowhere on the web they cannot reach. There is nothing they can't find or do if they are given access to a computer and internet. And the documentation Delaney creates makes it virtually impossible to tell if they're the real thing or not."

Turning toward nurse Rachel, Michael explained, "Cori is blind. However, she sees and hears more than she lets on. The Lord has granted her spiritual sight. Whether it is through dreams, or seeing what cannot be readily seen. Despite being blind, she sees more than anyone in this house…including Val."

Cori turned her head in their direction, seeming to see them standing there. "Kai, can you go get me some water, please? And Jerrod, would you please go get Jesse?"

"No problem," Jerrod said. He and Kai left for upstairs.

As soon as they were upstairs, Cori quietly said, "Michael, I see you. I also see two Rachels. I don't understand what's going on here."

"You are the only one who can see us," Michael explained. "We are on a mission of our own."

"The real Rachel is supposed to be upstairs sleeping," Cori said, her Irish accent still thick.

"She is," Michael acknowledged. "She is also here."

"I don't understand."

"Do not tell the others," Michael said. "This is a journey Rachel must go on by herself. She is not in danger."

"Yes, sir," Cori said, turning her attention back to the computer.

"What do you need?" Jesse asked, as he walked downstairs with Kai and Jerrod.

"I'm sorry. I got it figured out." Cori waved him off.

"All right. Let me know if you need me," Jesse said, and then went back upstairs.

"Here's your water," Kai said, setting it on the left side of her keyboard. He always set it in the same place.

"Thank you," she said.

"Now," Michael continued, "the crews down here keep communication lines secure. They also provide maps, get tickets, and provide any technical work needed for those on the field."

"Eagle to nest," Jacob's voice crackled over the computer's line.

Cori pushed the button on the microphone attached to the computer. "Go ahead."

"Do you have the extraction set up per our request?"

"Yes. Your tickets are at the airport. There are four. Once you land in Belize, the South America team will take over getting him under. They will meet you at the airport with your tickets for your flight home."

"Copy. Thank you."

"See you soon," Cori said, and then went back to typing on the computer.

"The man in question is running from the other side. He is only fifteen. Eventually, Senan will become an A.N.G.E.L. when he is old enough. We do not want them to bring him here, because they are already maxed. They are collecting those on the list to save them from the other side so we do not have a repeat of Aden Knight," Michael explained.

"If he is supposed to be on this team, why doesn't God just protect him?" nurse Rachel asked.

"He is. God used us to get him to safety," pregnant Rachel answered.

"I see. So, you're saying this God of yours uses people to do His work?" nurse Rachel asked.

"You're not a Christian?" pregnant Rachel asked.

"No. My dad wanted nothing to do with God, Jesus, or the Spirit. They remind him of my Uncle Nick."

"The uncle currently in the States," pregnant Rachel said in understanding. "Because Nico is not your dad in your reality, you were not raised in a Christian environment."

"Nope."

"Ladies, please focus," Michael said, putting his hands out. "Our next journey will take us to Ireland to see where Delaney, Cori, and Kai would be if they were not with the A.N.G.E.L.s."

One second they were standing in the bright lights of basement in the Haven…the next, they were in a dimly lit basement. The lights were blue, and the room was full of computers and various software. There were computers and screens everywhere.

"Cori and Kai are over there," Michael pointed out the pair on the other side of the room.

"Here are the travel papers you'll need for Ronan," Delaney said, handing them to Kai.

"You do seriously impressive work," Kai said, looking them over.

Owen walked into the basement. Snatching the papers from Kai, he scanned them. "Good job, Delaney. Cori, Kai, you need to set up a backstory online for him, so he can get into the facility."

"Working on it as we speak," Cori said, tapping away on her computer.

Looking over her shoulder, Owen read the backstory. "This is brilliant! You have all earned dinner for the next three days."

"Thank you!" Kai said, appreciatively. "That's generous of you!"

"Keep up this good work, and you'll continue to earn bonuses," Owen said, and then left the basement, papers in hand.

When he was gone, Cori stopped typing, and dropped her head onto her hands, shaking it. "Is there nowhere else we can live? There has *got* to be a better life then living in this basement waiting for Owen and his uncle to give us food. I feel like we're prisoners."

"In a way, we are," Delaney said. "We can't leave or they'll hunt us down and kill us."

"If we continue to stay, they may kill us anyway," Kai pointed out.

"Why would God abandon us?" Cori asked. "I know He's real. I know He's looking out for us."

"That darn free will," Kai said, shaking his head. "We made these choices."

"With our choices, comes good or bad circumstances," Delaney added.

Cori sighed as she went back to work on her computer.

RETURNING TO THE HAVEN, the three of them stood in the living room. "That was interesting," nurse Rachel said.

"Definitely!" pregnant Rachel agreed.

"Now, we will move to Mark and Derek," Michael said. "Here, they have been through a lot, but they are alive. In their younger days, they trained the next generation. Now, they serve as advisors to the teams."

"Derek's in a wheelchair," pregnant Rachel pointed out.

"Yes. However, he is alive," Michael reiterated.

"What does that mean?" nurse Rachel asked.

Putting his hands out, each girl accepted one, and they disappeared, only to be standing in a military graveyard a split second later.

"Nice," both Rachel's said with a shudder.

"Mark is over there, while Derek is over there," he said, pointing out their gravestones.

"Mark explained their gravestones were here anyway," pregnant Rachel said. "This doesn't mean anything."

"On the contrary," Michael said. "Because they were not A.N.G.E.L.s, there were many who were not rescued as they should have been. Both died on a mission several years after they earned and trained for their special operations position. They were not protected. They were also not followers of Jesus at the time of their deaths."

"Oh!" pregnant Rachel said, wide-eyed. "That's heart-breaking!"

"Now, because they died so early, Mark and Casey never met," Michael continued. "Because they never met, Jesse, Jon, and Angel were never born."

"Oh!" pregnant Rachel said, stunned.

"How does that affect me?" nurse Rachel asked.

"You never met your husband, nor had your children," Michael explained.

"I'm not married."

"Jesse is your soul mate," Michael said. "However, because Casey and Mark never met, and they never had their children, your soul mate is non-existent in your life."

"I see," nurse Rachel said, thinking.

"Since we are here in Denver, we are going to head over to look in on another factor to consider," Michael explained. Each girl grabbed a hand of Michael's and they disappeared, only to re-appear in Engine Company 15's common room. "Casey is over there," Michael said, gesturing toward Casey, who was in the kitchen cooking.

"She's still a firefighter?" pregnant Rachel asked.

"She never met Mark. Because the A.N.G.E.L.s do not exist in this reality, the other side did not hunt her down," Michael explained.

"So, it would have been better for her," pregnant Rachel said. "She was never tortured by Jacki."

"She *also* never found love again after Mac. She and Mark never connected. She never had Jesse, Jon, nor Angel."

"Shame," pregnant Rachel said, feeling a pit in her stomach.

"She still looks happy," nurse Rachel pointed out, as Jesse and Rob walked in from their ambulance call. They were joking and laughing with Casey, as they told a humorous story from their call.

"She may look happy here, but allow us to see the other

side," Michael said, taking each hand. They disappeared from the firehouse.

When they reappeared in the Haven, they were in the kitchen. Allie and Callie were helping Casey in baking more cookies for the kids to decorate. The kids were at the table. They would eat some cookies and decorate some cookies.

Looking at two of Leah's kids, Piper and Elijah, they all burst out in laughter. The kid's faces were covered in icing. "Oh! Your mom is not going to be happy with me!" Casey said, chuckling.

"We got it," Allie said. She and Callie each got a washcloth, and each one then wiped the face of one of the kids.

"There! That's better," Callie proclaimed. "Cute as buttons!"

"Want to help us with the popcorn next?" Jasper asked, as he, Ben, and some of the older kids were stringing popcorn. "It may be faster with more hands."

"That's only because with more hands, we're more likely to get them on the string, and not pop them into our mouths," Ben added.

"Agreed."

As the kids set to work on the popcorn and cookies, Kit went over to Casey, and leaned on the counter next to her. Fondly watching all the little ones at the table, Kit said, "Hard to believe we're grandparents several times over. It feels like yesterday we were running to Australia to get away from Lucca and Joey Rossi."

"That's right," Casey said, remembering. "Mark said he helped you escape when Joey went off the rails for you getting his brother Giovanni out from under his dad, Lucca. Giovanni turned state's evidence regarding their family."

"Yep. I wouldn't be here if it wasn't for Mark," Kit said.

"Oh no," nurse Rachel groaned. Dropping her head onto her hand, she shook it, dread written all over her body.

"What's wrong?" pregnant Rachel asked.

Nurse Rachel looked up at her, and admitted, "I have a sinking feeling I'm losing to this choice for a reality."

"What do you mean?"

"If Mark, who is dead in my reality, didn't save your Mum, then pretty much every child here does not exist in my reality."

"Not necessarily true, but a good point," Michael said.

"What do you mean by that?" pregnant Rachel asked.

"Allie and Callie *are* Mark and Casey's children," Michael explained. "They are their children by adoption, not by birth."

"Amber," pregnant Rachel said.

"Who is Amber?" nurse Rachel asked.

"Amber was their mum," pregnant Rachel said. "We had to rescue Allie and Callie from the other side when they were about seven years old. Calliope had plans for those two."

"Those two young girls who cleaned the icing off the kid's faces?" nurse Rachel asked.

"Yes," Michael said, putting his hands out. As soon as each girl accepted his hand, they disappeared from the Haven, and reappeared in the caves at Black Rock.

Pregnant Rachel shuddered as she looked around.

"What's wrong? Where are we now?" nurse Rachel asked.

"We're in Black Rock," pregnant Rachel said. "The other side kidnapped Allie and Callie for Calliope to turn them into Sirens."

"Into...*what*?" nurse Rachel's jaw dropped. "Wait! Calliope? As in mythical Calliope?"

Calliope walked into the cave where they stood, with Allie and Callie on her heels. "Now, girls, there are some young men I need for you to bring back to me. You remember what to do?"

"Yes, ma'am," Allie said.

"We sing our song, and they will be putty in our hands," Callie added.

"Yes. You two are quite the asset!" Calliope said, pleased.

"Whatever you desire. We are here to serve you," Callie said.

"It's actually our pleasure," Allie added, with a twinkle in her eye.

"Why are they acting this way?" nurse Rachel asked. "These are not the same two girls I just saw!"

"Yes. They are," Michael said. "They are under the spell of Calliope. When they were held, Calliope played mind games on them, making them trust her to keep them safe from the demons."

"Wait! From the *what*?" nurse Rachel asked, horrified.

"I am an Archangel of the Lord God Almighty," Michael said. "I stand before you with His blessing, wings and all, and you question whether demons are real?"

"Are they?" nurse Rachel asked.

"Rachel, where there is light, there is dark. Where there are angels, there are demons. There is a battle of good versus evil going on all around you, whether you choose to believe it or not."

"As for Allie and Callie, Calliope turned them into Sirens," pregnant Rachel explained.

"Are you bloody serious?" nurse Rachel asked, stunned. "All of this stuff exists for real?"

"Myths are based on some form of reality," pregnant Rachel pointed out.

"Calliope?" a demon asked, walking into the cavern with them. It stood to several feet tall. Its body was coated in blackish-red scales. Its talons looked like they could slice through a human in a heartbeat. Its yellow eyes darted about, making sure not to miss anything.

"Yes?" Calliope asked.

"Cassiusss wants to know if the girlsssss are ready?" it hissed.

"Yes. We will be right there," she said, and it disappeared.

Nurse Rachel shuddered. "C-can we get out of here?" she asked.

Michael put his hands out, so each girl accepted his hand, and they disappeared, only to reappear in an archeological dig in Egypt. The wind kicked up dust around them, but it did not bother the trio. They were impervious to the elements.

Seeing Spencer in the distance, pregnant Rachel put her hands on her hips, and asked, "He never came on the search for the other box, did he?"

Spencer's face was covered with a handkerchief, while he wore a set of safety goggles to protect his eyes from the blowing dust. Brushing off an artifact with a tiny brush, he then handed it off to an intern to catalog.

"No," Michael said. "He remains an archeologist. He never came on the search, because he never met Angel. He never had the delight of seeing the contents of the box."

"And, he never joined the team," nurse Rachel said in under-standing.

"Precisely," Michael said. "Do we need to see where Spencer is at in the other reality?"

"Why don't I just fill her in?" pregnant Rachel asked.

Michael nodded. "Go ahead."

She leaned forward in order to see nurse Rachel, as she explained, "He's one of the two couples getting married in a few days. He is marrying Katia."

"Oh," nurse Rachel said. "Who's Katia?"

Michael secured their hands into his, and they disappeared from Egypt, back to the living room in the Haven. Katia and Spencer were on the couch, looking at photos from a trip they took by themselves a few weeks ago. They were remembering their trip, as they excitedly discussed the upcoming wedding.

"That is Katia. She was adopted by Mark and Casey," Michael said. "Her sister, Liliya, is going out with Kai. You met him earlier," he said to nurse Rachel.

"The one who got the water for Cori?" nurse Rachel asked.

"You have a good memory," Michael said, pleased.

"Um," pregnant Rachel interrupted them, "if Mark, Casey, and the A.N.G.E.L.s weren't there to rescue Liliya…" her voice trailed, fear and concern written all over her body.

"What happened to Liliya?" nurse Rachel asked. "Or do I not want to know?"

Michael put his hands out. When each girl took a hand, they disappeared from the Haven, only to reappear in Sergei's basement in Russia.

"Where are we?" nurse Rachel asked, as her eyes adjusted to the lack of light.

"Sergei's basement," pregnant Rachel breathed out. "This is where he held Liliya."

"Where who did what? Why? What happened?" nurse Rachel asked.

"Liliya was kidnapped," pregnant Rachel said. "She was to be sold in a sex trade operation."

"That's it!" nurse Rachel declared, raising her hands in surrender.

"What's it?" pregnant Rachel asked.

"If you're telling me that innocent little girl will be thrown into that world if we choose my reality, I cannot in good conscious choose my reality. As if the other people's lives weren't enough, I won't even consider keeping mine with her life on the line," nurse Rachel said. "I give up. I choose her reality," she said, gesturing toward pregnant Rachel. "Knowing what I know now, with all of the evil that is literally crawling all over this world, I can't do it. Knowing that Jesus, God, The Spirit, and the A.N.G.E.L.s are real in the other reality, and not in mine, I can't go back. I won't do it." She crossed her arms.

"Do you agree?" Michael asked pregnant Rachel.

When pregnant Rachel did not say anything, nurse Rachel said, "You cannot be serious! Why is this even in question?"

"I am under *a lot* of pressure in my reality," pregnant Rachel defended herself. "It's a heavy burden to carry. That's not even adding in the children."

"You are blessed more than you know!" nurse Rachel said, bordering on anger.

"I know. I'm just…it's a lot," pregnant Rachel said, beside herself. "You have to understand."

"Well, let us take a look at the other Rachel's life, so *you* can see how *she* lives," Michael said, putting his hands out.

When the girls accepted his hands, they disappeared, only to reappear in nurse Rachel's condo. "This is where I live," nurse Rachel said, picking up her puppy. "This is Jesse."

Rachel just nodded, stifling her laughter.

"Go ahead and laugh," nurse Rachel said with a smile. "When I saw the real Jesse, I was stunned. You probably see my Jesse, and imagine your Jesse as a dog."

Pregnant Rachel could not help the laughter. "I'm sorry."

"It's okay," nurse Rachel said. "I get it."

"Please explain to her what your life is like," Michael said, sitting down on the couch.

"Well," nurse Rachel said, plopping onto her soft recliner, "I work twelve hours a day as head nurse over the entire shift. I'm on my feet, under beck and call for every nurse and doctor in the hospital. I *may* be able to grab a sandwich here or there, but I generally just keep a steady flow of caffeine at my fingertips. Then, on my days off, I go to the nursing facility to care for my dad, Nate."

"I thought Nate died?" pregnant Rachel asked Michael.

"He did in your reality. In this reality, he *did* attack Katie on her first visit, but since she never got out of Cleveland alive, Nate did not attack her again at the station," he explained. "He was never killed."

"I see," pregnant Rachel said, with multiple thoughts crawling through her mind.

"My mum died in a car accident several years ago. Pop's

been in the facility due to Alzheimer's. He, unfortunately, is nearing the end of his journey," nurse Rachel explained. "He hasn't recognized me for years."

"Isn't it heartbreaking to continue to go see him?" pregnant Rachel asked.

"It is, but he's still my dad. He may not know me, but I still know him."

"And, your brother?" pregnant Rachel asked.

"He does his own thing. Jake's a professional surfer on the circuit. He doesn't have time for the day-to-day stuff. I don't mind. He has an angry streak in him I don't particularly care for. In this reality, I'm alone."

"What happened to Serenity Wells Station?" pregnant Rachel asked.

"Nick still owns it. He's an Agent-in-Charge at the FBI, so he lives in the States. His mate, Pete, actually runs it. Uncle Nick is set to retire here soon. When he does, he'll come and run the station."

"Did he ever get married? Does he have any children?" pregnant Rachel asked.

"No. When Katie was killed, it broke him at his core," nurse Rachel explained. "He never found love again."

"So, when Nana and Pop died…" pregnant Rachel started.

"Nick refused to come back to Australia to run the station," nurse Rachel finished. "Pretty sure the station will be handed down to Pete and his clan once Uncle Nick dies."

Pregnant Rachel groaned, dropping her head into her hands. Shaking her head, she said, "I just wanted things to slow down a bit."

"Well, if we choose my reality, it'll come to a full halt," nurse Rachel pointed out. "You *have* to choose your reality. I cannot, for the life of me, figure out why this is even in question! Yours is *so* much better than mine! In yours, everyone's life is more enriched than they are in my reality. People are safer. You guys also help other people. Do you not see how your world is so much more in balance? What is wrong with you?"

"I don't know," pregnant Rachel admitted.

"Just say you agree with me," nurse Rachel pleaded.

"What say you?" Michael asked pregnant Rachel.

"I agree," pregnant Rachel said. "In seeing the two realities side-by-side, I have seen the undeniable difference." Looking at Michael, she added, "Will the Lord continue to bless us?"

"Of course. Just because you had a crisis of faith and needed assurance, does not mean He abandoned you," Michael said.

"Thank you."

"Since you both agree, please join hands," Michael instructed, as he stood. When they stood and joined hands, Michael said, "Close your eyes."

"Thank you for taking this journey with me," pregnant Rachel said to nurse Rachel.

"Thank you for the many sacrifices you and your team have made over the years," nurse Rachel said, and gently squeezed pregnant Rachel's hand.

Then they closed their eyes. Pregnant Rachel tried to catch her breath, as she felt like the air was sucked out of the room. She fell to the ground, curled up in a ball, and went unconscious.

# IT'S THE MOST WONDERFUL TIME OF THE YEAR

"*J*esse!" Rachel sat up in bed, screaming in horror. "Jesse!"

Jesse ran into the room. "Rachel?" He asked, resting his hands on the sides of her face. "Rach, are you okay?"

Breathing heavily, she said, "The other Rachel."

Jesse furrowed his brow. "What other Rachel?"

"The other Rachel," Rachel said, looking around. "Is she gone?"

"I don't know who you're talking about."

"She must be gone. Michael, he –"

"Michael? As in Michael, the Archangel?" Jesse asked, struggling to follow her train of thought.

"Yes. He…I'm fine," Rachel said. "What time is it?"

"You've only been asleep for about an hour."

"No! It was longer than that. We were –"

"What? Was it a dream?" Jesse asked.

"No. Michael showed me what life would have been like without Jesus and the A.N.G.E.L.s. It was not good," she said. "Everything was horrific. Those people downstairs all had completely different lives, *if* they were alive at all."

"I'm sorry. That sounds terrible."

"It was. It brings a real-life picture of how Jeremiah 29:11 works."

"What do you mean?" Jesse asked, sitting back a little bit, holding her hand.

"Jeremiah 29:11 says, *'For I know the plans I have for you,'* *declares the Lord, "plans to prosper you and not to harm you,* *plans to give you hope and a future.'* When He created the world, and we're included in that, He had a plan for each of us. He created the A.N.G.E.L.s to help aide in that plan," she explained. "Without the A.N.G.E.L.s in the world, and those who follow Jesus, the world will fall out of balance."

"Right. We know that."

"I forgot that," Rachel said. "I was too focused on balancing my responsibilities as Overwatch and being a mother, that I forgot that. I lost my focus. My focus needs to be on Jesus and doing His work. The rest will fall into place."

"This is true. Looks like that nap did you a world of good."

"It did," Rachel agreed. "Now it's back to the grindstone."

"No. Jerrod is taking over your duties as Overwatch until you're ready to come back...*after* the birth of the babies," Jesse said. "As for Charlie and Derek, trust me, there are more than enough teens and other kids down there to keep them entertained. The nursery is all set up. Christmas is your favorite holiday, and it's going on downstairs. Why don't you just enjoy the world around you while you put your feet up for the remainder of this pregnancy?"

"I think that's a wonderful idea," Rachel said with a smile.

"Great! Let's go!" he said, helping her out of bed.

What they walked into was chaotic, but fun. The noise levels were high, and there were people bustling in every direction, but they were filled with joy and laughter. There were stockings hung on the wall because there was not enough room on the mantle. Rachel knew there would never be enough room on the mantle. Remembering nurse Rachel's mantle with her and her dog's stockings, she was grateful for the chaos. The house was bursting at the seams with love.

"What do you want to do? Do you want to help the little ones do the cookies or string the popcorn with the teens?" Jesse asked.

"I think I'll do the cookies," she said. Together, they headed into the dining room. They sat with Charlie between them, and Derek on Jesse's lap, as they worked on decorating the cookies.

THE DAY ARRIVED for Scott and Stacey to land in Reno, Nevada. Jesse drove the van, while Spencer rode with them. Everyone else was still at the Haven, preparing for the wedding the next day.

"Why couldn't I stay and help?" Spencer asked. "I *am* one of the grooms."

"I realize that, but I need you to help me with these guests."

"Why?" Spencer asked. "Who are they?"

"It's a surprise for the couples. I'm afraid you won't know until they walk down the terminal. And no one else knows, except a few at the Haven."

"Interesting. Okay," he said stroking his chin, "you've piqued my curiosity. Do I at least get a hint?"

"Nope!" Jesse laughed. "You *do* get to know before any of the others, though."

"Fair enough. Do I get to know how many there are?"

"Two."

"Can I guess?"

"Oh!" Jesse laughed. "You'll *never* guess these two."

"Fine!" Spencer huffed, crossing his arms. "If you're going to be like that…"

"I'm going to be like that," Jesse confirmed.

***

"THIS IS THE TERMINAL, AND," Jesse glanced at the flight infor-mation, "their plane landed a few minutes ago. They should unload shortly."

Spencer and Jesse leaned on the railing at the terminal entrance. "I see some people," Spencer said, looking through the glass doors.

"Keep in mind, there are a few planes in. Just relax. Did you ever hear the saying, *curiosity killed the cat*?"

Spencer chuckled. "I can't help it. Curiosity in engrained in me."

"I don't know how you do it," Jesse said, thinking.

"Do what?"

"Do this without your family.

"I *have* family. The A.N.G.E.L.s are a bigger family than I ever dreamed of," Spencer explained. "Most of the family is in Michigan from my mom's side. Then, on my dad's side, it's pretty small. There was a divorce, which knocked out half that line."

"I see."

"Blood is important when it comes to closeness, but loyalty speaks volumes," Spencer said. "I mean, think about it. The Haven is bursting at the seams with family. I have more family than –" He stopped short when he saw his mom and dad walking down the terminal. A tear slowly crawled down his cheek.

"Yes," Jesse whispered. "It really is them."

"But, I didn't think – How did this happen?" Spencer asked.

"Angel and Rachel. Now, go to them." Jesse nudged him.

Spencer crawled over the railing, and met his parents just as they came through the doors. "Mom! Dad!"

Stacey dropped her bags. She ran to Spencer, throwing her arms around him in a hug. Jesse helped Scott with the luggage.

"Thank you," Scott said relieved. "I want to hug him too, but I can't with all of this luggage. You would think we were going to be here for a month with all she packed."

"Well, it's Christmas," Jesse said with a shrug. "The packing rules go out the window for Christmas."

"True. Plus, it's our only child's wedding," Scott added. "That alone warrants an extra suitcase. Though, I don't think she's going to let him go."

"It's just been so long," Stacey said, wiping her tears. "I'm not sorry! I don't want to let him go!"

"Let's get you all to the van," Jesse coaxed. "There are more who want to see them."

"Agreed," Scott said, shifting the bag on his shoulder. "Plus, I want to hug him too, but I can't until I get rid of these."

When they got to the van, Scott put the bags he was carrying down, and wrapped his arms around both Stacey and Spencer. They were all in tears…happy tears, but tears.

As they pulled into the long driveway of the Haven, Jesse warned, "Just so you know, there are a lot of people in this house. I know you're used to quiet, but it is far from that right now."

"That's okay. It'll be wonderful to spend Christmas with our son, his new bride, and all of you," Stacey said, as she and Scott sat in the second seat, holding hands.

"The wedding is tomorrow. Christmas Eve traditions start the next night. And then, it's one of the two most wonderful days of the year," Jesse said. "The day Jesus was born, and the other is day He resurrected, celebrated at Easter."

"Amen!" Stacey said. "This will forever be an amazing time of the year! We are blessed."

"Well," Jesse said, putting the van in park. Turning the van off, he turned toward them, and said, "please remember all we talked about when we go in there."

Scott narrowed his eyes. "What do you mean?"

"Just remember this great feeling," Jesse said. "There's a surprise in there."

"A good surprise or bad surprise?" Scott asked pulling the bags out of the van.

"Time will tell," Jesse said.

While everyone unloaded, Scott tried to ask more questions, but Jesse would not answer him. As they walked into the house, Spencer and Jesse stepped aside.

Stacey set the bag she had on her shoulder down, and looked up to see Kit walk out from among the sea of people. Stacey closed her eyes and shook her head. When she opened her eyes, she still saw Katie MacKenna standing in front of her. A much older Katie, but she was definitely Katie. Stacey closed her eyes and rubbed them. When she opened her eyes again, Katie still stood in front of her.

"Scott?" Stacey asked. "Please tell me you're seeing her –" she stopped short, when Nick walked behind her, resting his hands on Katie's shoulders. "Do you-do you see them?"

"Yes." Scott stared at them, dumbfounded. "I don't know how, but yes."

"We need to talk," Kit said.

"Why don't the four of you go into the study?" Casey suggested. "It's through those doors," she said, pointing to a set of double doors to the right of Scott and Stacey.

"Go ahead," Spencer said. "You guys need to have a long talk. We can catch up later."

While the four of them went to the study, Jon, Jesse, and

Spencer took their bags to what would be their room for the duration of the trip.

"I-I don't understand," Stacey said, as she and Scott sat on the couch. Nico and Kit each pulled a chair over to sit in. "You two got blown up in a van. We were at your memorial services."

"There *was* a funeral," Nico said. "I don't know if you remember, but Katie was being hunted at the time."

"I remember she was getting creepy messages and packages," Stacey said.

"Well, they were from Joey Rossi," Nico explained. "His father was head of the Rossi Family."

"As in *the* Rossi Family?" Scott asked. "As in the organized crime Rossi Family?"

"Yes."

"Oh boy," Scott said, shaking his head. "They are bad news. Joey Rossi is head of the family right now. Lucca died about ten years ago."

"Exactly. That's why Jesse and Rachel had you sign the non-disclosure agreement. If Joey had any idea Kit was alive –"

"You mean Katie," Stacey corrected.

"No. When we died," Nico made quotes with his fingers, "we got new identities. Katie's name was changed to Katherine. However, since it was too close to Katie, we decided to call her Kit for short. My name was changed to Nico. We decided it would be easier to remember our new names if they were close to our old ones."

"Good thinking. So, where have you been all this time?" Scott asked.

"On a station in Australia," Nico said.

"What have you been doing?" Stacey asked.

"Well, we have four children. One is Rachel," Nico said. "She has a twin named Leah. Then, there are two older twin boys, Joshua and Caleb. They're here too."

"*Two sets of twins?*" Stacey's jaw dropped. "Wow!"

"Yes. Josh is getting married tomorrow to a wonderful young lady, Zahra, at the same time Spencer and Katia get married. They're the other couple in the double-wedding," Nico told them. "Our other children are all married with children of their own. Jesse and Rachel have two young ones, not twins, and are having a set of twins. She's due in about a week."

"She said she was due on the thirtieth. I don't think she'll make it by her size," Stacey said, struggling to process seeing Kit and Nico alive and sitting in front of her.

"We don't either. Her twin sister, Leah, married Finn Walker. They have five children. Then, Caleb and Willow have two boys, and a set of boy and girl twins. Twins run in our family on both sides, so it wasn't a surprise that our children had them."

"That's crazy!" Scott said. "One was a lot of work. I cannot image having four of them."

"They are a blessing," Kit said.

Stacey took Kit's hand into hers. "I have to admit I'm upset regarding the duplicity, but I also understand. I only have one question."

"What?" Kit asked.

"Are you happy?"

Kit smiled. "Very much so."

"Good," Stacey said, relieved. "You went through a lot growing up. I'm glad the second half of your life was much happier for you."

"You always were gracious." Kit gave her hand a squeeze. "Do you forgive us?"

"I do," Stacey said.

"I do too," Scott agreed. "I have a question as well."

"What?" Nico asked.

"Since we signed the non-disclosure agreement, can we see Spencer more frequently if we don't tell anyone where we're going? I mean, he's getting married tomorrow. Who knows when they'll start having children? We'll want to be able to see them."

"That's something you'll have to talk to Rachel about," Nico said. "We're not in charge. She is."

"Fair enough."

Stacey gave Kit a hug. "I'm just grateful you're still alive. Can we keep in contact with you?"

"How much time do you guys have off a year?" Nico asked.

"We're going to be retiring soon," Scott said. "We'll have a lot more time on our hands then."

"We can plan it," Nico agreed. "We'll have Cori and Kai set it up. We'll also give you an email to use to get in contact with us."

"Thank you," Stacey said. "We're all getting older. We've lost other friends over the years."

"Anyone I know?" Kit asked.

"Well, Melody died about five years ago from cancer," Stacey said. "That one still hurts."

"Oh! She was so sweet!" Kit sat back in her chair. "I'm so sorry!"

"Brian took it hard. Their kids have carried him through. He's just now getting back to normal," Stacey explained.

"Kit had a bought with cancer, too," Nico pointed out. "It was touch and go for a while there."

"I'm glad you're still with us," Scott said.

"Me too," Kit said.

"We also lost Alex about twelve years ago due to a heart attack," Scott added. "Marissa was devastated. They weren't able to have children, so she leaned on the group to pull her through."

"How are Randy and Harmony?" Kit asked.

"They're enjoying life. They have a farm out near Amish country," Scott said. "Brian moved onto the farm when Melody died."

"Where's Marissa?" Nico asked.

"She's too into her city life in Cleveland to leave for the

farmland," Stacey said. "She lives about an hour from us. We're in between the two."

"Are you still in Pine Crest?" Kit asked.

"Yes. I actually work for the FBI Cleveland Office as a profiler," she explained.

Kit smiled. "That's perfect for you!"

"It's unique," Stacey admitted. "It was working with you, Nico, when our town was being fought over that I got the idea of working with the FBI come to mind. I am a profiler for them."

"Glad t' hear I had an influence," Nico said, pleased.

"You let me, Adam, and the other kids help. You believed in us, and taught us a lot."

"Thank you," Nico said. "I appreciate that."

Hearing a knock on the door, Nico called out, "C'mon in!"

Poking her head in, Rachel asked, "Everyone okay in here?"

"Yes," Nico said.

"It's almost time for dinner. We just needed to know if we should drag our feet."

"You guys go ahead and eat," Nico said. "I think we're going to be a little while. They're both still in shock."

"No worries," Rachel said, and left, closing the door behind her.

"I'm having a difficult time accepting the fact that you are sitting across from me," Stacey said. "When you died, it hurt big time! I'm not saying that to make you feel bad. I'm just saying I mourned."

"I'm sorry. I really am," Kit apologized.

"I understand. It was that or Rossi killed you for real. My mind is just blown a bit."

"Did Spencer recognize you from the wedding pictures when he saw you?" Scott asked.

"It took him a few times, but yes," Kit admitted. "We swore him to secrecy. I'm so glad you are allowed to know everything now. No more secrets."

"Agreed. I'm also glad we'll be able to see Spencer more," Scott said.

"How did you do it?" Stacey asked. "There were bodies. How did you get away with everything?"

"We had a lot of help," Nico said. "Scott's sister had two cadavers who matched our sizes pretty well. We blew the van up, which charred the bodies. Then, we got a private flight. It took many moving parts. We have had many interesting situations over the years, but God worked it all out."

"Yeah," Kit said. "Remember Dominic Cook?"

"From the diner on campus?" Stacey asked.

"Yeah."

"Yes! What happened to him?"

"Well, he got away from when he kidnapped me," Kit explained. "Then he came to Australia for our memorial and immediately recognized me."

"What did you do?" Scott asked Nico. "I would go ballistic."

"I very well could have," Nico said, "but that wouldn't have helped the situation. We decided to make it a *keep our enemy closer* scenario."

"What do you mean?" Scott asked.

"What did you do?" Stacey asked.

"We hired him."

"You did *what*?" Stacey's eyebrows arched in surprise.

"He was one of my favorite cooks," Kit said. "His food was always amazing!"

"That's beside the point," Scott interrupted her. "He kidnapped you!"

"He did," she said.

"However, it was better to know where he was, then to let him go," Nico explained. "By keeping him on the station, I could keep a better eye on him...and so could the ranch hands."

"Ohhh." Scott nodded. "I get it."

"Yeah. And he *was* a great cook! Over time, he also found the Lord," Nico added.

"Really?" Scott asked, surprised.

"Yep. God works in mysterious ways!"

"So, you guys have been on a ranch in Australia this whole time?" Stacey asked.

"Yes," Nico confirmed. "Kit's safe. The kids grew up in an environment safe and full of love, and, now they're A.N.G.E.L.s."

"That brings me to another question," Stacey said. "How do you stay sane knowing they're going throughout the world on these secret missions. Not knowing if he's even alive or dead when he can't have contact with us is killing me."

"I understand," Kit said. "Believe me. Here's the thing, God gave them to us. We raised them the best we could. The kids being one of the Lord's A.N.G.E.L.s makes me proud to know they're in His service."

"Is it safe? Not really," Nico admitted. "But what they do, and where they go, help people here on earth, and have eternal ramifications – whether good or bad. God had a plan for them way back when. Some of those kids, and I say kids because of their age comparison to us, but some of those kids stumbled onto this, and some were predestined. Either way, they do their job with the utmost efficiency. What they do changes lives."

"But it could cost them theirs," Scott countered.

"Matthew 16:25 reminds us, *'For whosoever will save his life shall lose it: and whosoever shall lose his life for My sake shall find it.'* To lose your life in the line of duty for the King of Kings and Lord of Lords is an honor! Those kids all understand the risks. Trust me. They've been through anything you can remotely think of – and some things you never even considered."

"So, what you're saying is God trusted them to us to raise, and now we need to trust Him to continue His work in their lives," Stacey said.

"Exactly!" Nico agreed. "You see, we're not in control. We were never in control. Control is a falsehood."

"What do you mean by that?" Scott asked.

"God created this world by His voice. He spoke it into existence. He owns cattle on a thousand hills. He knows the number of hairs on your head. He knows the number the grains of sand on the sea shore. He doesn't need anything from us. He gives us the blessing of allowing us to help others. When we do help others, it blesses us as much as them. When we learn we're not in control, and Who really is in control, taking our hands off the wheel is much easier."

"That makes sense." Scott nodded. "So, you're saying our kids are blessed by what they're doing?"

"Immensely! As a matter of fact, living they way they do, they are living on the edge, but they also are fully reliant on God."

"It takes Jeremiah 29:11 to the next level," Kit said. "They don't know where they're going or what they're walking into probably ninety percent of the time. They trust the One who's sending them."

"I can see that," Scott said. "Kind of puts things into perspective. While we don't go to foreign countries to help people, we can be a representative or an ambassador for Christ wherever we are."

"Oh! It goes much deeper than that," Kit said. "They're not just helping people. They are literally battling the other side."

"What do you mean?" Stacey asked, uneasy.

"They are literally battling demons, creatures of the dark, people possessed…the devil himself."

Stacey gulped. "Like right here in this world?" she asked.

"Yes," Kit said. "Like right here in this world."

"H-how does that work?" Stacey asked, heart racing.

"Just because *you* can't see them, doesn't mean they aren't operating in this world," Nico explained. "There are literal battles all over this planet. Just because demons are in the spiritual realm, doesn't mean they can't crossover into this realm."

Stacey shuddered. "That's scary."

"It is, but spiritual warfare is a reality many don't like to acknowledge," Kit continued. "They're fine talking about God, Jesus, The Spirit, and angels, but they neglect the other side. That's exactly what they want you to do. When you don't put on the armor of God, and you let your guard down, that's when they get you."

"I can see that," Scott said. "It's something we sort of faced in Pine Crest with the founding families."

"Oh! More than you know," Nico said. "I felt it when we stepped into your town. It was under a severe spiritual hold. Yes, the founding families were holding the town hostage, but what held the founding families?"

"Good question."

"Kyle," Stacey reminded him. "I wouldn't be surprised if there was a massive spiritual hold on Kyle. It's like he lost his humanity at an early age. He didn't think twice in doing what he did to us and the town."

"Exactly. The A.N.G.E.L.s call them unnaturals" Nico said.

"What are unnaturals, or do I not want to know?" Scott asked.

"They are people possessed. They look normal, until you send them over the edge, and then their eyes –"

"Turn black," Stacey cut Nico off.

"You've seen it?" Nico asked.

"Kyle."

"Seems we all have run into it at some point," Kit said. "We just don't always recognize it."

Scott ran his fingers through his blonde hair. "Guess we need to be more alert."

"I have to say when things are good, we tend to get comfortable," Stacey agreed. "We really do need to be more cognoscente of the spiritual realm of things."

"Agreed," Scott said.

"They were literally on the station," Kit admitted. "Like creatures of the dark, demons, unnaturals literally had a battle on our station with the A.N.G.E.L.s, ranch hands, Pete's clan, and the family."

"You're serious?" Stacey looked at her wide-eyed.

"We lost some good people during that time," Nico said. "Some *really* good people. The A.N.G.E.L.s have also lost some really good people through the years. Once again, they know the cost. They know to give everything they are, for everything He is. They also know it could cost them up to and including their lives on this planet. Here's the thing, though. As an A.N.G.E.L., The Spirit has given them each a special gift to help."

"Like what?" Scott asked.

"Well, Cori is a great example. She's literally blind."

"Where's Cori?" Scott asked. "What does she do?"

"She's one of their computer people."

Scott raised an eyebrow. "But, she's blind?"

"Yes. God, in His wisdom, has given her spiritual sight. She sees better than most of us. Val has the gift of spiritual sight as well. This has saved them time and time again. Jesse can feel the other side, and Rachel can look at you and tell you if you're one of the Lord's, seeking, or if you've given into the other side, or if you're working for the other side."

"Interesting gifts," Scott said, stroking his chin in thought.

"They are. They're not the normal spiritual gifts. These are specifically designated for the A.N.G.E.L.s," Nico said. "As Christians, we do have different gifts given to us by The Spirit."

"Right." Scott rested his arm around Stacey on the back of the couch. "So, you have all been living on the ranch, had an entirely new life, but it was happy?"

"Yes," Nico said. "We missed everyone, but Kit's safety was more important."

"I agree. I would do anything to protect Stacey. I get it."

"Glad you understand. Well, are you guys in a better head space now?"

"I think so," Stacey said. "It's still a little mind-blowing, but I understand."

"Same," Scott agreed. "It's a lot to take in, but I get it. I'm also happy we get to not only see Spencer, but also be present for his wedding."

"Are you ready to meet the rest of the family?" Nico asked.

"Definitely!" Scott said, and they headed out as a group to introduce Scott and Stacey to everyone.

THE DOUBLE WEDDING WAS STUNNING. Katia and Zahra were absolutely beautiful in their wedding gowns. The ceremony took place outside in the gazebo, and they were married by Mark, who took an online course several years ago. He got his license so there would be a legal minister at the Haven for marriages and burials.

The gazebo in the backyard was painted white, so they wrapped the railings with holly, tulle, and red bows. Katia and Zahra's bouquets were made of fire and ice roses, along with white and red roses throughout, and cascading ivy. The ribbons around the bouquet were silver, red, and green.

Katia's wedding dress was made with yards of beaded lace and appliqued tulle, with a ball gown floor-length skirt. The fitted silk bodice created a sweetheart neckline at the top, and flowed to the ground with an unbroken line. The beaded lace overlay on the bodice made it look like a sleeveless top. She wore her mid-back length hair down, with a flower wreath crown. The tulle of the veil hung down her back.

Zahra's bouquet and dress were both similar to Katia's. That was done on purpose. The difference was in the dress. Katia had the sweetheart neckline with a full skirt, while Zahra's had a princess scoop neckline with the lace only on the bodice. While Katia's was sleeveless, the lace overlay of Zahra's dress created a long sleeve effect. Zahra's skirt and a small train were created out of tulle, with a silk liner flowing to the ground. She also had a silver belt breaking the line of the dress at her waist. She wore her shoulder-length hair up in a French-twist, with wisps pulled down to frame her face. Her choice for a veil was a tiara, with the tulle down her back.

Since Mark was officiating and Zahra's family could not come, Jerrod walked Zahra down the aisle, while Jon walked Katia down the aisle. Katia went down first, followed by Zahra.

Both Josh and Spencer wore black tuxedos, with red ties and cummerbunds. They each had a boutonniere made with two fire and ice roses.

The ceremony was a beautiful, small wedding, attended by the family and friends present in the house. The two couples could not be more pleased on how it went.

During the cutting of the cake, both couples were kind, and kept it proper. Kai and Akio caught the garters, while Liliya and Hiro caught the bouquets.

After the ceremony, those adults in attendance stayed up longer than the kids and teens. They shared stories from over the years. Rachel cherished each memory shared, as she stayed on a lounge chair with her feet up. Her Braxton-Hicks contractions started at the beginning of the month. However, over the last two days, her contractions were real. They were still far enough apart she was not concerned.

"Tomorrow is Christmas Eve," Pete pointed out, as he sat down on the chair next to Rachel. Pete was the physician for Serenity Wells Station, and one of Nico's best friends. They were friends since Pete and Nico were children. Pete was the chief of his clan.

Rachel, Jerrod, and Liliya generally took care of medical issues at the Haven. However, in cases regarding childbirth, Pete held first right of refusal. He was there for the birth of all of the younger A.N.G.E.L. children. He was not going to miss Rachel and Jesse's last children, so he was at the Haven for the last four months in case anything went wrong. He came when they discovered Rachel was having twins.

"Yes. Yes, it is," Rachel agreed.

"How close are your contractions?"

"They're not. I should be fine."

"Just keep in mind that these are baby numbers three and four. They come quicker each time."

"I understand," Rachel said. "That's why I'm not up moving around too much. I'm trying to carry them to term. I'm not as concerned with Katie, as much as I am with Ethan. Boys develop slower in the womb. I want to give him the best chance possible."

"You've carried them longer than most. If they come a week early, I won't complain," Pete said. "Pretty sure you won't either."

"I won't," Rachel said in a chuckle.

"Rach? Are you going to stay up?" Jesse asked, coming over. "It's two in the morning."

"No. I was waiting for you," she said, putting her arms up for him to pull her up. "Night, Pete."

"Good night," Pete said.

After they said goodbye to Josh and Zahra, and Spencer and Katia, Jesse and Rachel went to bed. They knew the two couples would be leaving on their honeymoon in the early morning hours. Josh and Zahra were going on a seven-day cruise, while Spencer and Katia chose to go to Hawaii for the week.

THE NEXT DAY, the kids were difficult to keep contained. The excitement of Christmas, and being together, sent them over the top. The sugar of the candy canes and bottomless hot chocolate did not help. There were children everywhere of all ages. The teens did their best to keep them corralled and entertained with games through the day. By the time they little ones got down for their naps, even the teens took naps.

"Wow," Rachel said, sitting down on the couch, exhausted. "I'm thinking of joining them."

"How are you feeling?" Casey asked, sitting on one of the living room chairs.

"I'm fine. I've had contractions, but nothing productive. At least, I don't think they're productive."

"Are you feeling okay?" Pete asked, concerned. "I know you've been battling over the last few weeks."

"You have?" Nico asked, surprised.

"She has," Jesse confirmed.

"It's been rough," Rachel admitted. "I love all of our children, but I'm grateful these are the last two."

"I can understand your feeling on that," Kit said. "You love them with all your heart, but they are a lot of work."

"They are. And with none of them being school age yet, they're not quite ready for the independence they crave," Rachel explained. "I finally have Charlie and Derek out of diapers. We're heading into another few years of diapers again, and this time it's times two."

"That sounds exhausting!" Stacey said. "We only had Spencer. I cannot imagine juggling four of them."

"It *is* work, but it's worth it," Jesse said.

"Honestly, if it was just them, it wouldn't be so much to carry. With being Overwatch, it adds a lot more pressure and responsibility," Rachel said. "I'm thankful Jerrod stepped up to cover that for a bit. It was difficult with just one. With two at the same time, it's going to be a new rhythm to figure out."

"Honestly," Willow jumped into the conversation, "your two older ones will help out more than you think. Jasper helped out tremendously with Ben and Lily. Then, by the time Zach came around, Lily helped with him, while Jasper and Ben did their own thing. More kids sounds like a lot more work. Don't get me wrong, it is, but you have more hands to help."

"I can see that," Rachel said. "Allie and Callie helped with both Charlie and Derek."

"And, I'm sure all of the kids will help out wherever you need," Casey said confidently.

"I know. I need to tell you all about a dream I had a little while back," Rachel said. As they all listened, Rachel explained what happened in her dream regarding pregnant Rachel and Nurse Rachel.

By the time she finished, everyone was on the edge of their seat. "Honestly, the other Rachel reached her breaking point when we saw where Liliya was being held. After seeing what a difference Jesus and the A.N.G.E.L.s made in the lives of even other A.N.G.E.L.s, once we reached Sergei's basement, she was done."

"I don't blame her," Jacob said. He, Joe, and Delaney returned the day before the wedding in order to be back in time to attend. "There's no telling where I would be if it wasn't for the A.N.G.E.L.s. When you and Angel found me in the desert behind the house here, I was heading down the wrong path."

"I knew you guys were coming," Joe said. "If I didn't join you, I would probably be in a dead-end job. The A.N.G.E.L.s are my family. I found my wife in working with the A.N.G.E.L.s," he said, taking Delaney's hand into his.

"I know my life would be a lot less blessed," Val said. "There have been ups and downs since I became an A.N.G.E.L., but the ups massively outweigh the downs. I've been blessed to be a member of the A.N.G.E.L. family."

"You were in New Orleans," Joe said. "Didn't you have family there?"

"Sort of. There was a woman who took me in. However, New Orleans is a dangerous place to live, especially where we lived," Val explained. "With the A.N.G.E.L.s, I've been able to experience many different cultures, and had many people in my life who would not have been. I also have a true family in spirit and heart."

"Your life?" Nico said. "Hearing what my life would have been is depressing! I wouldn't have my wife, my children, nor my grandchildren."

"I wouldn't be a Christian," Rachel said. "The other Rachel was raised by Nate."

Nico shuddered. "That's just terrifying. The anger had such a stronghold on him, I'm sure he would have passed it down to the next generation."

"Well, in the dream, the other Rachel had a brother who was a professional surfer. She said he had an anger streak," Rachel explained. "My guess is it *was* passed down to the next generation. In taking out Nate, it took the anger out of the family."

"Life is full of choices," Kit said. "Those choices may seem minimal at the time, but in the grand scheme of things, some of those choices end up being the biggest ones of our lives. Those choices make us into who we are today."

"Agreed," Rachel said. "Each one of our lives were touched in major ways. Sometimes we forget that in the chaos of life. I'm grateful to not only the A.N.G.E.L.s, but also more importantly, to God, Jesus, and The Spirit. The Trinity changes more lives, hearts, and souls than the A.N.G.E.L.s could ever touch."

"Well said!" Mark said with a smile. "Without the Trinity, life would not be worth living."

"Amen!" Nico agreed.

"The environment here is like peaceful organized chaos," Scott observed. "I know with God at the center, life may be chaotic and stormy, but when you continue to focus on Him, peace will still reign in the chaos."

"Yes," Rachel said. "That's exactly what it feels like. In the dream, when we were looking at the other Rachel's life, there was no peace. There really wasn't anything. I felt numb."

"The darkness can overshadow and swallow you whole if you don't have the light of the Lord in it," Stacey said.

"Exactly!" Mark agreed.

"So, what is the plan for Christmas?" Stacey asked. "The two couples are on their honeymoon, but we're still here for a few more days."

"Oh! You're in for a treat!" Rachel said with a smile.

"On Christmas Eve, we sing Christmas Carols," Jesse explained. "After the carols, we each draw a name. Whatever name we have, we find one present under the tree with their name on it. On Christmas Eve, we get to open one gift. Then, on Christmas morning, we open the stockings and the rest of the presents."

"Don't forget the cupcakes," Rachel reminded him.

"I'm getting there," Jesse said. "After the present is open on Christmas Eve, we each light a candle, and sing the song *Gloria*. Afterward, we go to bed. Then the next morning, we read the Christmas Story from Luke 2. Then, we each have a cupcake with three candles in it."

"For breakfast?" Stacey asked.

"Yes. One time each year, we have a cupcake for breakfast. The cupcakes have three candles. The candles represent Jesus – He was, is, and always will be. We sing happy birthday to Jesus, blow them out, and enjoy our little birthday cake. After that, we open the rest of the presents and the stockings, and then breakfast. The rest of the morning is spent cleaning, cooking, and just having fun. We make calls to those who have family who are allowed to know about us, and then enjoy a feast. We snack for the rest of the day. Then, the day after Christmas, everyone fends for themselves. Since we have two little ones, we take care of them."

"Sounds like an honorable and fun way to celebrate the happiest time of the year!" Stacey said, excited.

"It is! And, it starts tonight," Jesse said.

"I can't wait!" Stacey grinned.

# O, HOLY NIGHT

That night, after the time of prayer, everyone dispersed for the night. Jesse and Rachel got Charlie and Derek down for the night, before heading to bed themselves.

"I love this time of year," Rachel said, brushing her hair, while Jesse brushed his teeth in the bathroom off their bedroom.

"Me too, I —" Jesse stopped short when Rachel gasped, and water dropped to the floor from under her nightgown.

Rachel looked up at Jesse, wide-eyed.

"Don't panic," Jesse said. "I'll get Pete."

He quickly rinsed his mouth from toothpaste. Rachel squeaked out in pain as she grabbed the sink. A contraction shot up in pain. She shut her eyes tight, as she tried to breathe.

"I'll get Pete. Breathe!" Jesse said, running out of the bathroom.

Rachel looked at the picture of Serenity Wells Station which hung in a frame between the sinks. She focused on the picture of the main house where she grew up. Breathing quickly until the pain subsided, she stood by the sink, not moving.

Pete ran into the bathroom with Jesse on his heels. "Rach?"

"It…is time," she got out in between breaths.

"Let's get you to the bed," he coaxed.

Rachel stood her ground. "No."

"Want me to go get Nico and Kit?" Jesse asked.

"Yeah," Pete said. "I don't think she's going to cooperate with me. She may with them."

"I can hear you!" Rachel growled with gritted teeth. "I'm right here!"

"I know." Turning to Jesse, Pete said, "Please go get Nico and Kit. I don't think it will take long for the whole house to know what's going on. I want to get her to the bed to get her comfortable."

"Don't…touch me!" Rachel snapped. She clutched the sink so tightly, she thought she might break it. "So…much…pain!"

"You've been through this before," Pete said, resting his hand on hers in an attempt to loosen her grip. Jesse ran for Nico and Kit. "You can do this," Pete coaxed. "That's why I've been here for so long. I figured they would come early."

"Pain!" she seethed.

"I know. We need to move you to the bed. It will be more comfortable."

"I don't –"

"Rachel." Kit walked in with Nico and Jesse. "Please let us move you to the bed. It'll be more comfortable for you. I will not lie to you. It's going to hurt beyond measure, but you are bringing two little ones into the world. I can honestly say I know how you feel."

"I…know…you do," Rachel said between breaths. She still had one hand on the sink, her other hand held her stomach.

"Then, please let me help you through this?" Kit offered.

Rachel just nodded, so while Jesse and Kit helped Rachel to the bed, Pete and Nico ran downstairs. Nico got Casey and Stacey up to help, while Pete worked in the kitchen to get ready.

"We need to wake the others to pray," Stacey said, walking in with Scott.

"I agree. While I'm sure you are all perfectly capable to do this, God is the Great physician," Scott said.

"I agree. Would you please get Jerrod? I want both of you to help me with this birth," Pete said to Scott. "I know you are a paramedic, and Jerrod is a former Corpsman. I can use all the help I can get."

"Agreed," Scott said, and disappeared down the wing where the A.N.G.E.L.s slept.

"We have a lot of work ahead of us tonight," Pete said to Stacey. "It's going to be a long night."

⚜

"Ahhheeee!" Rachel screamed at the top of her lungs. A few of the A.N.G.E.L.s already moved all the sleeping children into the wing where the A.N.G.E.L.s slept, so they would stay asleep.

"You're ten centimeters, Rach. Push when you feel the urge," Pete encouraged.

It was twenty minutes to midnight. By that point, Rachel was in labor for over three hours. The contractions started hard once her water broke, and never let up.

"I don't know how much more of this I can take!" Rachel said when the contraction finally subsided, tears pouring down her cheeks.

"You can do this, sweetheart," Jesse said, feeding her ice chips.

"Oh, I remember why I didn't want to do this again," Rachel groaned. "Another one!" she said in a growl.

"Really? Already?" Pete asked, eyebrows arched in surprise.

"Yes!" Rachel said, and growled. "Need...to...push!"

"Go ahead. We're ready," Pete said, and then looked to Scott, who would take the first baby to clean. Scott nodded in response, and grabbed a clean pillow case to hold the baby when it came.

Rachel pushed for fifteen agonizing minutes, before their little girl was pushed out into the world.

"It's a girl," Pete announced. "Jesse, come cut the cord."

After Jesse cut the cord, Pete handed the little girl to Scott, who took her into the bathroom. They set up a heat lamp to keep the babies warm while they cleaned them. He rested her on the changing pad on the counter, and then proceeded to clean her off.

Rachel lay back on her pillow, breathing heavily. "Is she okay?" she asked, hearing her crying in the bathroom.

"Yes," Scott said from the bathroom. "Ten fingers and ten toes. Color is good too."

"Okay, now for number two. Whenever you are ready," Pete told Rachel.

"Just give me a few minutes?" Rachel asked.

"That's up to him," Pete said. "Sorry to say we're all on along for the ride at this point."

Rachel nodded, while Jesse gave her more ice chips. When she finished what was in her mouth, she turned to Jesse, and said, "I want to change her middle name."

"Why? And to what?" Jesse asked.

"She was born on Christmas Eve. What if we name her Katherine Noel?"

"I think that's a beautiful name," Jesse agreed. "I think that's a great idea."

"Have one for the boy too," Rachel said.

"What's that?"

"Ethan Christian," Rachel said. "He'll probably be born on Christmas day."

"I think that's a fine name," Jesse said. "Let's do it."

"Thank you. I...I-eeee!" Rachel said, screeching in the middle of the sentence as a contraction spiked without warning.

"Number two is on the way," Pete announced. "Ready, Jerrod?"

"Ready," Jerrod said with a nod, holding the second pillow case.

Rachel pushed for thirty agonizing minutes, even tearing as he burst into the world. Pete handed the little boy, who was screaming at the top of his lungs, to Jerrod. Jesse cut the cord, so Jerrod could take the little boy to the bathroom to clean him. Scott walked out with little Katherine Noel a few moments later.

"Want to hold her?" Scott asked.

"I will," Jesse said. "Pete's stitching her up."

"Also getting the afterbirth," Pete said, pressing on Rachel's stomach.

Jesse took the little girl into his arms. Rachel's heart overflowed with love at seeing the little girl in her daddy's arms.

"He's a healthy little guy," Jerrod said, walking in with little Ethan Christian. "A healthy set of lungs, too."

After Pete finished, Jerrod handed Ethan Christian to Rachel.

Rachel held her little boy in her arms, as Jesse sat down on the side of the bed with Katherine Noel in his arms.

"Beautiful family," Michael, the Archangel, said, suddenly appearing in the room with nurse Rachel by his side. "One born on Christmas Eve, and the other born on Christmas Day."

"You're here?" Rachel asked, stunned.

"I wanted to show her she made the right choice," Michael explained.

"It's a beautiful picture," nurse Rachel said, admiring the family.

Charlie and Derek burst into the room, accompanied by Kit. "I thought they should be here," Kit said when Rachel raised an eyebrow.

The two boys climbed onto the bed to see their new siblings. Charlie went to Katherine and Jesse, while Derek went to Ethan and Rachel.

Wiping the tears from her eyes, nurse Rachel said, "That is what was missing. Love."

"That love comes from the acceptance of the pure love Jesus shared with this world when He came all those years ago. He gave up His place in Heaven on a night like tonight. He came, so the world could live. He gave everything. When we give everything we are, for everything He is, our lives have new meaning," Nico said, standing on the other side of Michael. "Rachel told us about the two different realities. The difference between the two was Jesus."

"I knew I made the right choice," nurse Rachel said. "To see this only solidifies that choice. The difference between the two worlds is clearly evident."

Nurse Rachel looked toward the family on the bed. When she and Rachel made eye contact, Rachel mouthed, *"thank you,"* to nurse Rachel.

Allie lightly knocked on the door.

"Come on in," Rachel called. "Everyone's decent."

"We came to sing to the little ones," Callie said, walking in with Allie, Jasper, Ben, Lily, Zach, Sophie, Piper, Elijah, and the A.N.G.E.L.s who were home, minus Akio and Hiroaki, who were watching Sebastian and Conner. With everyone in the room, the young ones sang, *O, Holy Night.* Halfway through the song, everyone joined in:

"O, holy night the stars are brightly shining.

It is the night of our dear Savior's birth.

Long lay the world in sin and error pining.

'Till He appeared and the soul felt its worth.

A thrill of hope the weary world rejoices.

For yonder breaks a new glorious morn.

Fall on your knees.

O, hear the angels' voices.

O, night divine.

O, night when Christ was born.

O, night divine, o, night.

O, night divine.

A thrill of hope the weary world rejoices.

For yonder breaks a new glorious morn.

Fall on your knees.

O, hear the angels' voices.

O, night divine.

O, night when Christ was born.

O, night divine, o, night.

O, night divine."

"Very appropriate," Rachel said. "Thank you!"

"We wanted to welcome the Christmas A.N.G.E.L.s into the world," Allie explained.

Michael, the Archangel, took the moment and quoted John 1:9-14, and John 3:16-17: **(John 1:9-14)** *"The true light, which gives light to everyone, was coming into the world. He was in the world, and the world was made through Him, yet the world did not know Him. He came to His own, and His own people did not receive Him. But to all who did receive Him, who believed in His name, He gave the right to become children of God, who were born, not of blood nor of the will of the flesh nor of the will of man, but of God. And the Word became flesh and dwelt among us, and we have seen His glory, glory as of the only Son from the Father, full of grace and truth."* **(John 3:16-17)** *"For God so loved the world, that He gave His only Son, that whoever believes in Him should not perish but have eternal life. For God did not send His Son into the world to condemn the world, but to save the world through Him."*

# Christmas Wish

By:

## C.J. Peterson

# BONUS STORY - CHRISTMAS WISH

***The Christmas Spirit***
**"Glory to God in the highest, and on earth peace, good will toward men." Luke 2:14**

"*R*obin! Come on, sweetheart!" her grandmother called, with her strong southern drawl. Being in deep east Texas, the accents were thicker than near the cities. Everyone on the Flynn side of the family had it. The little girl's mother's side was from Mexico, so the Spanish accent was laced through each of her family members on that side. Blending traditions of both sides of the family around the holidays made for a fun time. "Time for dinner!"

Six-year-old Robin Flynn crashed through the back door, giggling as she ran in. "Hi, Grams!"

"You're so cute," her grandmother said, pinching her cheeks. "Dinner's on the table. Go wash your hands."

"Momma and Daddy aren't here yet," Robin said, concerned. "Are we eating without them?"

"Yes." She knelt in front of Robin. Tucking a portion of the young girl's raven-colored hair behind her ear, she explained,

"Your mama's in the hospital. Your new brother is coming soon!"

Excitement lit Robin's face. "Really?"

"Yep! So, I need you to help me with Christmas this year. Usually your momma and daddy do, but your daddy got home from the oil rig this afternoon and went directly to the hospital. He wanted to see you, but he needs to be with your momma."

"What can I do?"

"You can help me frost the cookies I've been baking all day. We're going to deliver them to some friends of mine. I know they would absolutely love to see your bright, smiling face when we deliver them."

"Sounds great! Be right back!" Robin said, and took off for the bathroom. Scrubbing her hands, she could not get her mind off her mom, and the baby who would soon join the family. She hoped with every bone in her body they would both be okay. She had a friend who lost his mom when she went to the hospital to have a baby last school year. She remembered how heartbroken he was when he finally returned to school. She did not wish that feeling on anyone.

After dinner, Robin and her grandmother frosted the cookies, while her grandfather separated them into different tins. As he closed each tin, he placed a bow on top. "There!" he said satisfied, after putting the bow on the last tin. "All set. Erin, do you need me to drive?"

"If you want to, we would enjoy the company. Just make sure to bring your cell phone in case Brandon calls," Robin's grandmother, Erin, said. Then, as she packed the tins into a sturdy box, she reminded him, "We need to hurry. We have Christmas Candlelight service tonight, Elijah."

"Got it. You have the list in delivery order?"

"Always."

"Are we going to sing Christmas songs?" Robin asked, as her grandfather left to get the car.

"No. I think just a visit will do. We have several deliveries to make. Besides, we'll sing Christmas songs tonight at church," Erin explained, closing the flaps of the box. "Hopefully these won't slide."

"Erin!" Elijah called from the living room. "The car's ready when you are."

"Can you help me carry these?" Erin called back.

"Of course," he said, coming into the kitchen. Before he helped with the box, he knelt in front of Robin, and explained, "We're fixin' to visit some older people tonight. All I ask is you be the respectful and sweet little girl we know you are. When your daddy comes to get you in the next few days, I want to give him a good report."

"I will, Pops!" she said with a grin.

Robin was a people pleaser, yet a bit of a free spirit. She enjoyed exploring the world, and everything it encompassed. One of things she cherished the most was the time she and her dad spent together in the shed behind the house. Her dad worked on the oil rigs, so when he was home, he wanted to spend as much time with his family as he could. In order to spend extra time with Robin, therefore giving his wife, Andrea, a break, he let Robin stay with him while he welded. Sometimes he helped a friend by fixing something. Other times, he created works of art made of metal. Anytime she was in there, she had to wear her welding helmet. Her dad gave it to her two Christmas's ago. It had flames of various shades of red, orange, yellow, blue, and white, tipping at the end with a light purple...her favorite color. Her name was painted in a deep purple. She loved and adored her father, and the talent he possessed.

⁂

THEY WENT TO SEVERAL HOUSES, before arriving to the house her grandmother said was for her best friend Cora. Robin got out of the car, anxious about meeting someone so close to her grand-mother. Her grandmother said not to worry, that Robin met Cora when she was a baby, but obviously, Robin did not remember.

When the older lady opened the door, a smile spread across her kind face. Her white hair was kept short, and she walked with a cane. She was considerably shorter than her Grams. Robin instantly liked her sweet personality, as she stood there in a blue housecoat with white flowers.

"Hello!" Cora greeted them. Looking down at Robin, she asked, "Who might you be?"

"Cora, this is our granddaughter, Robin Flynn," Erin said with a proud grin, and a twinkle in her blue eyes. "She's joining us this Christmas, as her momma's in the hospital having her little brother."

"I should have known by the pictures. Hello, Robin! What a beautiful young lady you are! And a new baby? How exciting!" Cora clapped her hands together. "I'm so happy for you! You're going to be a big sister!"

Robin could not help the smile on her face. "Thank you!"

"Do you know what your little brother's name will be?"

"No." Robin shook her head. "Momma said they wanted to wait to tell everyone."

Presenting the tin of cookies to Cora, Erin said, "We stopped by to bring you your regular Christmas treat."

Cora accepted the tin, and gave Erin a hug. "Always a pleasure, Erin. Thank you."

Hearing the phone ring in his pocket, Elijah pulled it out and answered it, "Hi, son! Are we grandparents again?...What's wrong?...I see. Sorry to hear that. We'll be right there."

Hearing her grandfather say, *"What's wrong?"* Robin's heart raced. *Was her mom okay? What about her brother?*

"Okay. Keep us posted," Elijah said. He hung up the phone, tucking it securely back into his pocket.

"What's wrong?" Erin asked.

"The baby's not in the right position. They're going to see if they can slow the contractions and try to manipulate the baby into the right position," Elijah explained. "They may have to do a cesarean section."

Erin gasped, coving her mouth.

"Oh!" Cora said, startled. "Would you like me to pray for her?"

"I think it would be a good idea," Elijah said, shoulders slouched. Turning to Erin, he added, "Deliveries will have to wait. We need to go to the hospital."

"Wait!" Cora said, and disappeared into the tiny, white and blue colored cottage-like home. She returned a minute later with a small bag. Her ninety-year-old, frail hands passed the bag onto Robin. When Robin gave her a quizzical look, she explained, "I'm not as good as I used to be, but my grandchildren and great grandchildren like to color the pictures I draw. I tend to have them on hand for when they come. I put a some in the bag, along with a wide variety of colors of crayons. I also added a few blank pages for you to make some pictures for your momma, daddy, and baby brother."

"Thank you," Robin said, accepting the bag. A thrill of excitement coursed through her body. Her baby brother was on the way!

After giving Cora a hug, they immediately headed toward the hospital, lost in their own thoughts.

***For Unto Us A Child Is Born***
**"Therefore, the Lord himself shall give you a sign; Behold, a virgin shall conceive, and bear a son, and shall call his name Immanuel." Isaiah 7:14**

ONCE TO THE HOSPITAL, Erin, Elijah, and Robin headed to the waiting room. Erin set Robin up at the coffee table in front of Elijah before she took off to go find Brandon and Andrea.

While she was gone, Robin set to work coloring the pages Cora drew. The first was a picture of a little baby in a hay box. While Robin colored it, she was confused as to why Cora drew a picture of a baby in a barn. The parents looked down at the little baby with love. There were a few other people in the barn with them, along with various farm animals. There was a bright star above, shining down on those within its wooden walls. Everyone looked peaceful as the adored the little baby.

Coloring the tiny boy with the sheep, she scrunched her nose, imaging the smell. Her great uncle lived on a farm. He died two years ago, but Robin still remembered the stench of the dairy farm.

Moving to the three men who looked like kings, she colored them with brilliant colors of red, blue, maroon, purple, and gold. She used gold on the trinkets they held, because they looked important.

When she colored the parents, she took caution to ensure the peaceful looks on the parent's faces remained intact. She loved how they looked so sweetly at the baby. She colored the mother's clothing light blue, and the father's clothing tan and brown. She wondered what the mom was thinking as they sat in the barn watching their baby stirring around in the hay.

Once she finished that picture, she moved to the next. It was of the side of a hilltop. There were sheep and shepherds throughout the field. She colored the grass green, and made sure each shepherd had different color clothing. For the little sheep, she chose white for their fuzzy parts, black for their noses, and peach for their faces. For the sky, she colored around the edges of the sky dark blue, followed by a lighter blue, and then she mixed yellow and white where the angels lit the sky in song. The angels all had different color hair, and while some had blue eyes, others had brown. She enjoyed creating the details.

"Do you mind if I visit with you?" a man asked, sitting on the couch across from Elijah.

"Who are you?" Elijah asked.

"I am Cora's pastor. She called and mentioned your daughter-in-law needed prayer. She said she was having trouble with the birth of the newest member of the family. You can call me Pastor Josiah," he said, shaking Elijah's hand.

"Pleasure to have you join us," Elijah said. "We are concerned. We go to church on Christmas and Easter. I know about this God of yours. Can He help?"

"That's my prayer," Pastor confirmed.

"Since we have time, care to tell me a little more about this God of yours?"

"Do you know the story about his birth?" Pastor asked.

"I've heard pieces during the Christmas Services over the years."

"May I?" Pastor asked Robin, pointing to the pictures she colored.

"Sure," she said, handing them to him.

"Do you want to hear the story too?" Pastor asked.

"Yes! I love stories!" Robin agreed. She climbed onto the couch with her grandfather, cuddling into him.

"Well, on a night much like tonight, there was a young pregnant woman and her husband. They were going back home, due to a census being taken. A census is where they count people. They did this regularly. Now, this lady was pregnant, but not by her husband."

"What? Did she cheat on him?" Robin asked, wide-eyed.

Elijah chuckled. He gestured toward Pastor to explain.

"Well, the young lady's name was Mary, and her husband's name was Joseph. Before they were married, Mary was visited by an angel, who told her she would have a baby. She was pregnant before the marriage. Now, back then, times were bit different than they are now. Mary did not cheat. If she did, Joseph could have done many bad things. However, he was visited by an angel of God, too. Because of that visit, he chose to keep her as his wife."

"So, where did the baby come from?" Robin asked.

Elijah chuckled again, and looked to Pastor. When Pastor raised an eyebrow, Elijah said, "You started it. She only six. Good luck answering that one."

Pastor had to smile at Elijah's comment. "Well, God gave her the baby," Pastor said.

"How?" Robin asked.

"The best way to explain it is that the Holy Spirit blessed Mary, and then she had a baby in her tummy." Before she could ask again, he pushed forward with the story. "Anyway, they went to a tiny town called Bethlehem. When they got there, they didn't have much money. And since there was a census, all those people visiting stayed in the hotels, called Inns back then."

"So, where did they stay?" Robin furrowed her brow. "She was having a baby. Why wouldn't people let her have a room?"

"Joseph continued to search, finally landing at the last Inn on their list. When the Inn owner said there wasn't any room, Joseph was desperate. Mary was struggling. The time for the baby was almost here."

"Kind of like your momma," Elijah said. "Remember how your momma kept having tummy pains?"

Robin nodded. "Yes."

"Mary was having the same pain," Pastor said. "Joseph begged the Innkeeper. He even said a stable would do. A stable is a barn."

Robin perked up. "Like the picture!"

"Yes," Pastor said, happy she started making the connection. "So, the Innkeeper felt for the couple, and let them stay in the stable. Well, while this was going on, there were shepherds in the fields, watching their flocks."

"The other picture!" Robin said, excited to understand the pictures Cora drew.

"Yes," Pastor said, holding it up. "See? The shepherds watched the sheep to make sure no one or no bad animals got to them."

"Neat!"

"So, that same night, the shepherds were doing what they normally do, when all of the sudden, the sky lit up! God's angels started singing!"

"That's cool!" Robin said, on the edge of her seat. "What did they do?"

"At first, they were afraid, until one of the angels explained the Messiah was born, and all they needed to do to find Him was follow the star."

"This star?" Robin asked, pointing toward the bright star over the stable.

"Yes."

"Then, is this one of the shepherds?" Robin asked, pointing to the young boy in the stable picture.

"Yes," Pastor said, pleased once again she made the connection. "For such a young lady, you're very bright."

"My momma says I'm too smart for my own good," Robin quipped.

Pastor and Elijah burst out in laughter.

"I don't doubt it," Pastor said.

"Who are these guys?" Robin asked, pointing to the ones she thought were kings.

"They are wise men from the east. They knew The Messiah would –"

"What is a Messiah?" Robin asked, cutting him off.

"A Messiah is the promised One, The King. Through time, it was rumored The Messiah would come and save the nations.

This story had been going on for so long, some thought it would never happen. Meanwhile, these three wise men saw the signs from the story, and they made the journey. They brought gold, frankincense, and myrrh as presents for the baby's birth. There is a problem with this picture, though."

"What?" Robin asked.

"The picture is wrong. They did not find The Messiah, named Jesus, until He was probably a little over a year old. When the wise men got to Bethlehem, it was long after the night of His birth. They went to the king of the land to ask about the baby. When the king found out, he got angry. He didn't want anyone to steal his throne."

"I don't blame him!" Robin said, wide-eyed. "I wouldn't want anyone to take my castle either."

"Exactly. He did some bad things due to his anger. The wise men, being smart, finally found Mary, Joseph, and Jesus in Nazareth. The wise men were warned not to go tell the king where they found the baby in a dream. So, after they gave their gifts, they left. An angel warned Joseph in a dream about the bad things the king would do, so they packed up and left for Egypt until it was safe. The little family got out just in time."

"Good!" Robin said, relieved. "That poor baby had a bad enough time being born in a stinky stable. He didn't need a king angry with Him, too!"

"I agree! Now, over the years, this young child grew in strength, and was very smart about the Bible."

"What's the Bible?" Robin asked.

When Pastor looked to Elijah, Elijah explained, "Her dad wants nothing to do with the church. That's a story for another time, though."

"Got it. Well, the best way to describe the Bible is a love letter from God."

"God? As in the One who created the world?" Robin asked.

When Pastor looked to Elijah again, Elijah shrugged, and

said, "Sometimes we can get a few stories in here and there. We cheat."

"Fair enough," Pastor said. Turning back to Robin, he explained, "Yes. When the Bible was written, God told the men what to write down. He gave the words to those who wrote the different books in the Bible. So, when you read the words of the Bible, you are reading His words."

Robin smiled. "That's neat!"

"Yes. It is. Now back to our story. Jesus grew. He listened when they went to the temple, which is another name for church. He soaked in the words He heard. He was wise, sometimes smarter than those in the temple. People were shocked at what He said at times."

"My momma says she's shocked sometimes at what comes out of my mouth," Robin said.

Pastor and Elijah broke out in laughter once again.

"You are truly a delight," Pastor said to Robin.

"So, is there more to Jesus's story?" Robin asked.

"There is, but it may be a bit scary for you," Pastor said. "We may need to save that for another time."

"Planting seeds may eventually see growth," Elijah said knowingly to Pastor.

"Agreed," Pastor said.

Elijah and Pastor talked, while Robin colored some more. After a little bit, Pastor left, only to return about twenty minutes later. "Robin, will you and your grandpa please come with me?" he asked, with a sack in his hands.

Curious, Elijah went with Pastor and Robin. They stepped outside and sat on a stone wall. Once settled, Pastor opened the sack. He pulled out a cupcake for Robin and handed it to her.

Elijah raised an eyebrow. "Isn't it a little late in the evening for that?"

"I have a feeling y'all will be up pretty late tonight," Pastor said. "I've already been to her room."

"Fair enough," Elijah agreed.

Pastor handed Elijah a cupcake as well. Then he pulled his own from of the bag. Afterward, he pulled a small box of candles, placing three candles on each of their cupcakes.

"Why three candles?" Elijah asked, curious. "At candlelight service, we only have one."

"The candlelight service, and this, are two different things," Pastor said.

"What do you mean?"

"This cupcake is in celebration of Jesus's birth," Pastor clarified. "You see, the candles represent Jesus – His past, present, and future."

"What does that mean?" Robin asked, while he lit the candles.

"Jesus is the Son of God," Pastor explained. "He was always here. Way before the world was even created, He was there. That's His past. He always is. In other words, He is here with you, just as he was with people in the past, and will be in the future. This is His present. He will always be here until His return. Lastly is His future. He always will be. When I die and go to Heaven, Jesus will be there with me forever. He will be with all of those who are His into eternity in Heaven."

"So, He is around right now?" Robin asked.

"In a good way, yes. I am one of His. I follow Him. I worship Him. As one of His, He looks after me and takes care of me."

"How does He do that? Isn't there a lot of people who follow Jesus?" Robin asked.

"That question is bigger than me," Pastor admitted. "Your mind is fascinating. You are an amazing young lady, who has an incredible future."

"Thank you," Robin said. Looking toward the melting candles, she asked, "Are we fixin' to blow the candles out?"

"Yes. But we need to sing *happy birthday* first," Pastor said.

"After all, tomorrow is when we celebrate His birthday. It's nine o'clock. I feel it's close enough to His birthday to celebrate it."

"Christmas is His birthday?" Robin asked, studying the flames on the tops of the candles.

"It's when we celebrate Jesus's birthday. Let us sing," Pastor said.

Together, they sang *Happy Birthday*. Afterward, they blew out the candles, and enjoyed the cupcakes.

"Do not worry about your mama," Pastor encouraged. "I've prayed for her and the baby. I know they'll both come through healthy."

"That's my Christmas wish," Robin said, finishing her cupcake. "I wish for a brother born on Christmas. I wished for Momma and Papa to be happy."

"I'm sure they will, little one," Elijah said, wrapping his strong arm around her tiny shoulders. "I'm sure they will."

***The Magic Of Christmas***
**"For with God, nothing is impossible." Luke 1:37**

MIDNIGHT CAME AND WENT...NO baby. Robin wanted to see her parents so badly, it hurt. She did not want to sleep in case something happened. She did not want to miss the birth of her new brother. Whenever her eyes went to close, she would hear a noise, and think it was them. She would jump to her feet in anticipation, only to be disappointed.

"What's taking so long?" Robin huffed. "We haven't seen Momma, Papa, or Grams for a long time."

"This is true. But it will be worth it when we do," Elijah said, hugging the little girl closer. "Why don't you nap. I promise to wake you when your little brother comes into the world."

"There's so much noise here," Robin complained, leaning her head on her grandfather.

"Let's try this." He adjusted her so her head lay on the couch near his legs. He covered her with his jacket to make her toasty warm. She was out in seconds.

Seeing his wife come into the waiting room about thirty minutes later, Elijah slowly got off the couch. Pulling Pastor with him, they met her near the desk, out of earshot from Robin.

"She's having trouble. They're taking her in to get a cesarean section," Erin said, hands shaking. "I-I don't know what to do here. I'm afraid. Brandon's stressed beyond measure."

"I cannot imagine what you're feeling," Pastor said, lowering his voice, resting his hand on her shoulder.

Hearing a tiny voice, they all jumped. They separated to see Robin standing there rubbing her eyes. "What happened to Momma? Is the baby okay?" she asked.

Kneeling next to her, Pastor said, "I have faith God will look after your mom and little brother."

"Will they be okay?" she asked, almost understanding what he did not say.

"We pray they will be," Pastor said.

"Yes. They will both be fine," Erin corrected.

"Lord willing," Pastor said.

"He'd better!" Erin snapped.

Pastor's heart broke for her. "I've been praying all night for Andrea and the baby to both come through healthy."

"When I blew out the candles, that was my wish too," Robin said. "My Christmas wish is for Momma and the baby to be okay."

"I'm sure they will be, sweetheart," Erin said, picking her up, hugging her.

"It shouldn't take too long if they're heading down now," Elijah pointed out.

"They've been down for a little bit," Erin said. "I had to go outside to get some air. She was in so much pain before they finally took her down." She wiped the tears from her eyes. "I don't understand why they waited for so long. They let Brandon go into the operating room with her."

"Let's sit while we wait," Pastor said, gesturing to their spot for most of the evening on the couches. Together, they sat down, all lost in their own thoughts and feelings. Robin sat on the floor using the coffee table to color some more, while the other three talked quietly amongst themselves to distract from what was going on just a few floors down.

AROUND TWO IN THE MORNING, the doctor walked into the waiting room. Seeing him, the trio and the Pastor arose from their positions, anxiety written all over their faces.

"Is-is she okay?" Erin asked. "Andrea. Is she okay? Is the baby okay?"

"They are," the doctor said. "I want to keep them here for a few days. With a cesarean section, that's normal. I want to make sure there is no infection, and that the baby continues to improve. As you know boys develop at a slower rate than girls. With the baby being born a week early, that concerns me. He seems to be doing okay, but I want to make sure he continues to grow in a healthy way."

"Thank you. When can we see her?" Erin asked.

"Give her a few, and I don't see why not. She's exhausted, but I'm pretty sure she wants to see this little one," he said, gesturing toward Robin.

Seeing her father walk into the waiting room, Robin squealed in excitement. "Daddy!"

She ran into his arms, and he scooped her off the ground. "Hey, little one!" he greeted her in a hug as he spun her around. Adjusting to look into her eyes, he smiled, as he said,

"Guess what? You're a big sister now. You have a little brother."

Robin squealed again, wrapping her arms around his neck. "That was my Christmas wish!"

"Want to go see Mommy?" he asked.

"She can, but I ask the others to wait for a bit before going back," the doctor said, and then left the waiting room.

"Okay. Let's go," Brandon said, carrying Robin. Talking to her on the way back to the room, he said, "He's adorable. You're really going to like him. You can't see him just yet. They're making sure he's going to be okay."

"What's his name?" Robin asked.

"We're naming him Steven Jesus Flynn, but we're going to call him Stevie. His first name is after my uncle. His middle name is after your grandpa on your mom's side. Little Stevie has black hair like yours, and dark brown eyes like yours."

"Like Mommy's hair and eyes."

"Yeah," Brandon said with a chuckle. "I know I'm your daddy. You're so much like me, it's crazy. I would love to see one of you at least have my light brown hair and blue eyes. Having said that, I thoroughly enjoy seeing your mother in your features. You're the spitting image of her. You know that, right?"

"Yes. You always say I'm as beautiful as she is."

"Inside and out," he agreed. "Well, here we are," he said, pushing open the door.

The light blue room had machines beeping, while her mother had an IV in her arm, dripping at a steady pace. Tucked under the white blankets in the hospital bed, she looked so peaceful. The curtains were closed, protecting her sleep from the sun when it would rise in a few hours. There were only a few lights on, keeping the room dim.

"Mommy?" Robin asked, nervous when her mom did not open her eyes.

"She's tired. Give me a second," he said, setting her down on the ground. He kissed Andrea's cheek. When her eyes fluttered open, a smile crossed her face. "Good morning, beautiful," Brandon said to his bride.

"Hey," she said, weakly.

He gestured toward Robin. "You have a visitor."

"Come here, little one," she said, reaching her hands out toward her daughter.

Robin cautiously made her way to her mom. Reaching up, she held her mom's hand.

"Here," Brandon said, helping her onto the bed with her mom.

Robin took a moment to get comfortable in her mother's arms. Once she did, she instantly fell asleep.

"Oh, my little angel," Andrea said, stroking her hair. Glancing up at Brandon she asked, "How's Stevie?"

"They'll bring him down after they've checked him out," Brandon explained, gently sitting on the side of the bed.

"Knock, knock," the nurse quietly said, pushing the door open. "I have a visitor for you."

"Do we wake her?" Brandon asked, as the nurse wheeled Baby Steven's bassinette into the room.

The nurse mentioned to call when it was time to come get him to take him back to the nursery, and then left.

"Baby." Andrea gently shook Robin. "Robby, honey, your brother's here."

Robin's sleepy eyes opened. "He's here?" she asked.

"He's here," Andrea said.

Brandon picked up the baby from the bassinette. He then gently set him in Andrea's arms. "He's beautiful," Brandon said. "Just like his mother and sister."

"Can I touch him?" Robin asked.

"Yes, honey. Go ahead," Andrea encouraged.

Robin reached over and rubbed her fingers on his tiny arm. When she got to his hand, he wrapped his itty-bitty fingers around her finger. "Guess what, brother?" Robin asked. "You are my Christmas wish. You will be a blessing to many, as the other baby did who was also born on this day," she said and kissed his head.

"Who are you talking about, honey?" Andrea asked.

"She's talking about Jesus," Elijah said, coming into the room with Erin and Pastor Josiah.

"I don't want to talk about Jesus right now," Brandon said, jaw clenched. "I want to focus on my children and wife."

"Jesus wants to give you peace," Pastor said. "Looks at the gifts He's given you in these young ones, and your wife. He has blessed you tenfold. Christmas Day is the perfect day to talk about Jesus," Pastor said.

"And a perfect day to come back to Jesus," Erin hinted. "Give *yourself* a gift this year."

"Make it *your* Christmas wish, Daddy," Robin encouraged. "The story is really neat!"

"If you want to talk, I'm here," Pastor offered, presenting him with his card. "All you have to do is call."

"Thank you," Brandon said, tucking it into his wallet. "Maybe one day, but not today."

"Is that a promise?" Pastor asked.

"It'll be *my* Christmas wish…when you're ready," Erin said, holding Elijah's hand. "In the meantime, let's enjoy this little gift."

"They're *both* a gift," Andrea said.

The little family bonded, and enjoyed the precious gift in little Steven. They also enjoyed a plate of cookies frosted by Erin and Robin. After that, Robin used the pictures to tell her mom about the story Pastor shared with her, while her dad watched from the chair, holding Stevie.

***Peace On Earth***
**"Come to me, all you who are weary and burdened, and I**
**will give you rest."**
**Matthew 11:28**

IN THE EARLY MORNING HOURS, while Stevie was still in the nursery, and Andrea and Robin were sleeping on Andrea's hospital bed, Brandon called Pastor Josiah. Pastor agreed to meet him in the peaceful garden in the courtyard of the hospital. That way Brandon was still close to his family.

As he sat down on a bench in front of the pond to wait for Pastor, he noticed the fish in the Koi pond. He also noticed the water lilies floating on the water, and the various insects that flew from one water plant to the next. The dragonflies danced on the waterfall cascading down the rock wall. The beauty and peace did not escape him. The Christmas trees and decorations in the hospital did not escape him either. There was beauty all around him, but inside of him, there was trouble.

"I'm glad you called," Pastor said, taking a seat next to Brandon.

"I'm sorry for messing up your Christmas morning."

"To talk to someone about Jesus will never mess up my Christmas." Pastor waved him off. "It's my honor. Watching the sunrise on Christmas morning is always a treat. Watching it while discussing my Savior makes it that much sweeter."

"Does your family feel the same?"

"They know what our true work is here on this earth."

"You speak as if earth isn't your home," Brandon observed.

"In all honesty, it isn't."

"What does that mean?"

"I'm a child of God. I'm a prince in His Kingdom. This is my temporary home. I'm looking forward to eternal rest when it's my time. Until then, I'll live on this planet, but know my home is in Heaven."

Brandon dropped his head into his hands, shaking it. "I wish I had that peace."

"Tell me," Pastor said. "What's so heavy on your heart, that even on this beautiful Christmas morning, where you have a new baby and a wonderful family, that you're still in turmoil?"

"You have a way with words," Brandon said on a sigh.

"Talk to me. You called me here for a reason."

"I don't know where to start."

"How about why you're so angry with Jesus?"

"He's supposed to love and care for those who are His, right?"

"Right."

"He's supposed to protect them from everything, right?"

"Wrong," Pastor said.

Brandon's eyebrows arched. "What do you mean?"

"Jesus walks with us. He protects our mind and soul, for those who are His. Our bodies are temporary. No matter what you go through, when you trust in Him, He will protect your heart. The world may come against us, but we are to never lose hope in Him."

"I'm afraid I still don't understand."

"Do you remember your history?"

"I'm pretty good with history."

"Then you are aware Christians were killed all through time after the death of Jesus, including right now, just because they choose follow and worship Him."

"What do you mean right now? I thought that stopped long ago."

"Do you not pay attention to the news? Christians are still being killed even today. Maybe not in America, but it's true in other countries."

"Why doesn't God stop it? Can't He just snap His fingers and stop it?"

"He can, but He's given us free will. With that free will comes dire consequences at times."

Brandon huffed. "Yeah. I know."

"What happened?"

"I don't know if I can say it aloud."

"You have to. You've been carrying this for a long time. I can see that."

"It hurts to talk about it."

"It hurts to carry it," Pastor countered. "I don't feel you were at fault."

"No. However, she and I got into a fight before she got into the car. The last thing I said to her was that I never wanted to see her again."

"Who was it?"

"When I was in high school, I dated a girl named Tara. I saw her and her friends flirting with a couple of my teammates. We got into a fight about it, and she took off. She left with the two girls she was with all night. On their way home, a drunk driver lost control of his vehicle and hit them head on. I found out about it as soon as the game ended."

"Oh no," Pastor groaned, dropping his head.

"There were no survivors. She was a Christian. I fell hard. I could never understand why didn't God stop it?"

"I'm sorry. I cannot answer that," Pastor said. "What I *can* answer, is that if she was a Christian, then she's at peace with God right now."

"She's at peace, but I'm not."

"That's because you're struggling inside. You're trying to make sense of something that will never make sense. I meant it when I said you've been blessed tenfold. However, you're living in the past, instead of the present," Pastor explained. "Your life has not been easy. Working on an oil rig is not an easy place to work. While we talked last night, one of the things Robin mentioned was how the two of you work in the shed when you're home. She loves it. She feels it's a great way for you guys to have fun. That girl adores you."

"I know she does."

"And your son will adore you as well. I have faith in that."

"But?" Brandon asked, sensing that was the next word.

"*But* what are you teaching them? When there's something you disagree with, you shut out the One who loves you the most?"

"What does that mean?"

"Your Mom and Dad told me you turned your back on Jesus in high school. Now I know why. The pain you carry is heavy. You have to get rid of it. You have to give it to God. You know she's at peace. You know she is in the best place possible…at the feet of Jesus. Why do you continue to carry the anger?"

"I don't understand why He let it happen in the first place."

"God is a God of love. He is a God of kindness and justice. When Jesus came to this earth, He came to provide a sacrifice which saves all who follow and believe in His name. You know John 3:16 and 17, right?"

Brandon rolled his eyes. "Pretty sure *everyone* knows John 3:16."

"They tend to, but they often forget verse seventeen goes with it. Mind if I quote them?"

"Go right ahead."

"*For God so loved the world that He gave His one and only Son, that whoever believes in Him shall not perish but have eternal life. For God did not send His Son into the world to condemn the world, but to save the world through Him,*" Pastor quoted. Then he continued, "You see, Jesus came to save this world. After He died on the cross, no more sacrifices needed to be made to atone for sin."

"I'm aware of that."

"Romans 10:9 tells us, '*That if thou shalt confess with thy mouth the Lord Jesus, and shalt believe in thine heart that God hath raised him from the dead, thou shalt be saved.'* Have you ever asked Him to be your Savior? Have you ever confessed your sins to Him, and asked Him take those sins from you?"

"Yes."

"Then, once you do that, you know you are one of His. Right?"

"Right. That doesn't help my issue."

"Ah, but I'm not done yet."

"What am I missing?"

"Hebrews 4:16 says, *'Let us therefore come boldly unto the throne of grace, that we may obtain mercy, and find grace to help in time of need.'* Did you take it to the throne and give it to Him?"

"I did. He didn't answer."

"Oh, I'm sure He answered. You may not have liked the answer, but rest assured, He answered."

"How do you know?"

"He always answers. The answer may be *yes*, or it may be *no*. It may even be *wait*. At any rate, rest assured He *does* answer."

Brandon heaved a heavy sigh, watching the dragonflies playing tag on the waterfall.

"There's still a lot in there," Pastor said.

"There is."

"And the turning point was the loss of Tara," Pastor said in understanding. "I'm going to hazard a guess, and say you've been carrying around a lot of guilt for the fight?"

"Yes."

"You have to know what happened to her was not your fault. You were not the driver behind the wheel."

"She was upset."

"She was on her side of the road, according to you."

"She was," Brandon agreed.

"Then, how can you claim responsibility? Last time I checked; you were not in control of the world."

"No. God is. He let it happen."

"He gave us free will."

"That darn free will," Brandon said on a sigh.

"Yes. It has its good points and its bad points. Tara was upset. She chose to get behind the wheel, instead of talking to you. Do you agree?"

"I hate it, but I do," Brandon relented.

"Now, the drunk driver chose to get behind the wheel, instead of taking a taxi. Do you agree?"

"That one I agree with wholeheartedly."

"That's because it fits your narrative."

Brandon furrowed his brow. "What do you mean?"

"You want to hate someone. You want to blame someone. God is at the top of that list. You thought He should do or not do something, so you're choosing to put the blame on Him, instead of on whom it should be placed."

"Which is who?"

"Tara and the other driver."

A heavy silence hung in the air. Finally, Brandon said, "Anyone ever tell you they hate you?"

Pastor smirked. "All the time."

"You're too logical."

"I have a lot of life experience. I've learned the hard way, and wish to not have others learn this way. God has taught me many lessons over the years. I've lost my fair share of people. I questioned God many times, just as you have. I learned to give it to God."

"I did."

"Then you took it back. Instead of laying it down and leaving it there, you chose to grab it before you left, and have carried it for all of these years."

"Hate to say it, but I agree with that."

"Your mother's Christmas wish was for you to lay it down, and leave it there. She wants you to be free from carrying that burden," Pastor said, resting his hand on Brandon's shoulder.

"I know it is."

"Then, let me help you fulfill that wish. Let the Father give you the gift of peace this Christmas."

"Now *that* would be *my* Christmas wish."

"Why do I sense doubt?"

"Because I've been carrying it for so long."

"Exactly. Don't you think it's time to put it down?" Pastor asked.

Brandon sat silent. Deep in his own thoughts, he weighed his options for ten long minutes. "All right," he finally said. When Pastor did not respond, Brandon continued, "You've made compelling arguments. I'm not fully ready to trust Him yet, but I'm willing to give up the anger against Him regarding Tara."

"Wonderful!" Pastor said, pleased.

Together, they prayed. Brandon gave the incident regarding Tara to God. When he did, he felt a heavy weight come off his shoulders.

"Now, since God gave you a Christmas present of freedom, you need to give your mom the gift of letting her know her Christmas wish was granted."

"I agree. I'll let her know when she gets here. Thank you, brother," Brandon said, shaking Pastor's hand. "Now, go spend the rest of Christmas with your family."

They stood. Pastor hugged Brandon. "God is good."

Brandon hugged him back. "All the time."

For the rest of the day, he felt free. It was a feeling he had not felt in a long time. He enjoyed his family. He shared his gift with his parents, who were thrilled beyond words. This would go down in his book as his best Christmas ever!

# BOOKS BY C.J. PETERSON

**Grace Restored Series can be found: https://cjpetersonwrites.com/ series-books**

**Holy Flame Trilogy can be found: https://cjpetersonwrites.com/ series-books**

**Divine Legacy Series can be found: https://cjpetersonwrites.com/ series-books**

**C.J.'s Stand-Alone Books & Anthologies She Participated in can be found:**

**https://cjpetersonwrites.com/stand-alone-%26-anthologies**

**'Tis The Season, A Holiday Anthology is due out: OCT2021**

**Sands of Time Trilogy can be found: https://cjpetersonwrites.com/ series-books**

**Out of Time (Sands of Time Trilogy, Book 3) is due out JAN2022**